EYEWITNESS!

EYEWITNESS!

TIFFANY THAYER

CUTTING EDGE

ISBN-13: 978-1-962896-85-6

Published by
Cutting Edge Books
PO Box 8212
Calabasas, CA 91372
www.cuttingedgebooks.com

TO JUNIOR
who saw some of all
this happen.

PART ONE

CHAPTER ONE

Z im took three soft steps backward into the blackness of the smelly doorway and eased his rod out of its under-arm holster. A step at a time, leisurely and with apparent unconcern, the law approached, twirling its night stick at the end of a leather thong.

Zim's eyes narrowed and focused upon the shining spot that was the officer's badge. One, two, three, four—he counted the long easy steps.

On the other side of the ill-lit street two men in ordinary attire descended the steps of an apparently vacant house. One of them cleared his throat with artificial harshness. The law stopped and regarded the two, then whistling softly, turned, crossed the street and talked to them.

They *were* on then. The tip-off had been straight. He was in for it. Well, if there was going to be any double crossing he'd surely make it interesting for them—for a while anyway.... Until the truck gets by.

Until the truck gets by. Zim began saying that over and over again. Like the French soldiers repeating: *They shall not pass.*

Until the truck gets by.

The Boss had slipped him a century note, squeezed his hand and said, "I'm riding with the boys on the Mack tonight. They'll come in over the viaduct.... I just got it from headquarters that there's been a shake-up and that they want me.... You know they'll never get me alive. Not with this Baumes Law working."

"They wouldn't dare," Zim had argued.

"Nobody knows, Zimmy.... They say there's been a shake-up—and new men put in. Until we get to the right ones again we ain't any of us safe. But here's the dirt.... You hang around those warehouses just east of Taggart's old saloon. Smell around there off and on all evening—after eleven.... Don't get the bulls watchin' you—but keep your eyes open. We'll be through 210th Street before one."

Zim did not interrupt again. The Boss always knew what he was doing. And he never liked to be interrupted when he was giving orders. Slight as he was, he was hard, and Zim respected the edged tone in his voice, the quick, sharp brain that worked behind those piercing eyes more than he would have a brawny fist or a wide, piano-mover's back.

"If you see a special car or a congregation of cops, stick close enough to make trouble, but don't get into none. Wait. Wait it out until you hear us comin'—then start somethin'. See? Break a window. Snatch a purse. Shoot in the air. I don't care much what you do—as long as it ain't dangerous—and as long as you don't get caught. See? Don't let 'em catch you, not with no iron on you. All I want is for you to attract attention until the truck gets by. See?"

Until the truck gets by.

The harness bull moved away from the two dicks as if he had just been passing the time of day. A long, black touring car came slowly down the street, slowed to pick up the two men and continued its way toward the corner, where it stopped. The policeman ignored the car's presence and pulled his box on the corner.

Zim strained his ears for a sound of the approaching truck. It was after one. He listened as hard as a man may, shifting his weight and stretching his neck to avoid the soft scratch of his coat collar against his ear. Had the Boss changed his plans and come in by a different route?

A trolley bumped along two blocks away and out of its distant and diminishing thunder there came the low, even roar of a big Mack driven at high speed.

Zim looked at the car standing with running motor only thirty feet away. It was full of the law—and armed to the teeth. The patrolman was back on his side of the street, behind a telephone pole. His hand switched nervously under his blue coat tails and came back into sight grasping his revolver.

Zim had waited too long. The roar of the truck was close now. Guns were in readiness. The driver of the police car was clutching his wheel, his feet set for the sudden rush and chase that seemed inevitable. He had waited too long to draw them off with some harmless ruse. No matter what he did now, they would let the roundsman only chase him. They were too thoroughly keyed to get that truck.

Until the truck gets by.

He must do something desperate. They must all be made to chase him, and at once.

Zim raised the automatic and pulled the trigger. The uniformed officer leaped, turned and crumpled at the foot of the telephone pole as the familiar horn of the speeding truck sounded a warning to some pedestrian only a block away. Zim waited long enough to see four men leave the car, headed for the wounded policeman.

Until the truck gets by.

He stayed his anxious feet another moment. None of the men had seen his gun flash. They stood staring stupidly around them, not knowing where the shots had come from. Two more men crawled out of the car. They were exposed now, but they were also fully armed and their fingers were tightened around death-dealing triggers. One more from him and a pound of lead would whistle at his head. There was nothing else to do. The truck was almost there. They would all turn upon it unless he drew their fire.

He pulled again and tried to use his small Savage like a machine gun, mowing at the bulk of men before him as if to lay them all low. Then he ducked and ran.

Lights were appearing in windows. Inquisitive heads were being poked out all along the street. Up the steps he ran, trembling. A fusillade splintered the doorway below that was still warm from the impress of his body. A man in a night shirt stood before him in the hall.

Crash! His automatic descended full into the sleepy face. Then an idea came from nowhere and Zim dragged the heavy, unconscious body through the open door from which the fellow had emerged, and shut it behind him.

A woman's voice, tremulous with fear, came from a room beyond. "What is it, Henry? What on earth is it?" Zim was stealing a night shirt. It wasn't easy. The man's elbow stuck and delayed him. He threw his hat under a sofa, mussed his hair, drew the night shirt over his clothes and swiftly removed his shoes and socks.

The truck had gone by.

CHAPTER TWO

eavy feet pounded up the dark stairs, then paused. Above the heads of the officers all was black and still. They were not prepared for this. The only flash-light was still in the car. No electric buttons appeared on the grimy plaster walls.

"Hey." One of the cops hammered on the door at Zim's ear. "Wake up in there…. Where's the lights?"

Zim held his breath.

"Better get a flash," said one of them.

One was quicker to follow that suggestion, affording temporary safety, than either of his two fellows. He was on the street in a trice, running toward the car. The other two whispered—and waited.

The woman who had spoken to "Henry" puffed out of bed and waddled heavily through the familiar darkness of her home. Zim held his automatic behind him, in readiness.

"Why don't you answer the door, Henry? What is it?" she whispered.

"Sh-h-h," said Zim.

"A hold-up?"

Zim was afraid to so much as "sh-h-h" again. Complete silence. What next? He had no plan. He had little ammunition. The street would be filled with police and curious people attracted by the shooting. In another minute he would be entirely cut off from the roof—if he had ever had access to it. This little fat woman might discover his deception any second—might stumble upon her unconscious husband. And *he* might revive—would inevitably revive in a short time.

If he faced these men in the hall—now, any one of them might recognize him. It looked like his only chance. They might *not*. If there had been a shake-up, as the Boss had said, these might be new men, men who did not know him.

There was a faint groan at his feet. "What was that?" the woman asked.

Zim ventured one more "sh-h-h" and stepped to the door. Henry was coming to. Not until he had opened the door a crack did Zim remember how dark the hall was. Then he stepped half-way out, the better to display his white night shirt.

"What is it, officer?" he asked hoarsely, attempting to put the utmost respect into his tone.

"There's a gunman in the building. You better stay in there 'til we get 'im. We'll need you for a witness, maybe, later."

Lord! That was something else again. He'd be in the round-up of the residents. But he could not go back into that house now. The woman would surely discover him—and Henry...

Zim pulled the door shut behind him in defiance of the law's suggestion. "Where'd he go?" he asked, as he heard the footsteps of the flash-light bearer returning.

"He ran upstairs. You get back inside. There may be more shootin'."

"My God," Zim breathed and tried to efface himself in the shadow that led away from the stairs toward a window over-looking the street. That was a normal move—and it would take him away from the flashlight. He stepped to the window and looked out. Two men lay motionless in the center of a crowd. A third sat near them, rocking with pain and clutching his shoulder. One or two hardy souls peered into the dark hallway past the guard.

Behind him he heard the three officers start stealthily up the stairs, throwing a beam of light ahead. Quickly he darted to the stairs that led to the street. He might be able to fool the guard—some way. Two steps down and a piercing scream came from the room he had so recently left. Hope fled—then returned with a rush. There was his excuse—cut and dried. He slipped his gun back under his arm, pulled the collar of the night shirt tight around his neck and ran down stairs.

"Where the hell y' think you're going?"

"A doctor. My God! I've got to get a doctor, quick!"

"Y' can't go out like that!"

"But a man has been murdered."

"There's police up there, they'll take care o' that."

Four or five men crowded close to hear this interchange.

"What is it, Mac?"

"Is he up there?"

"Have they got 'im?"

"Oh, God, officer—just let me run across the street to the doctor. My brother's been killed."

"If he's dead the doctor ain't gonna do him no good."

"Maybe he can save him. He ain't dead yet."

"Shirt tail an' all?"

"Yes—this ain't no time to care."

"Go ahead!"

It had worked. Like an antelope, Zim gained the far curb and the steps of the empty house that had sheltered the federal men earlier in the evening. In the protection of the dark doorway he shed the night shirt and rolled down his trouser legs, refilled his automatic, and barefooted, walked to the rear of the house.

The chase would be still hotter in a minute. The woman must have disclosed his ruse by now. At least six people had seen him distinctly. He must have shoes. Damn a town that had no alleys.

He felt his way along the blind brick wall of a tenement and emerged thirty feet from the empty house. Turning to his left he almost collided with a huge negro, the janitor of the tenement.

"What's all de shootin', Boss?"

"A man just killed his wife," Zim said, edging behind the man.

"They ketch 'im?"

"Yes. They got 'im."

The butt of the automatic caught the negro just back of his ear. He swayed and sat suddenly on the cement stoop. A woman leaning from her window two floors above had witnessed the entire incident. She screamed. Zim transferred the janitor's shoes to his own feet, as a wildly gesticulating and arguing group moved toward him from the doorway across the street. Only the fact that the janitor had not laced or tied them in his haste to get to the street to view the rumpus permitted the shoes to be transferred in time.

Zim ran for it, zigzagging toward the far corner as fast as he could tear. The police opened fire. He rounded the corner without feeling a hit and continued to run—faster and faster. His nerves were shattered. They had a car. They would separate and surround him. There were no by-paths, no short blocks. The next corner seemed miles away. He dare not attempt another hallway nor an entry between buildings. There were blind pockets which would lead—eventually—to the chair. On, on, on. Around another corner, bullets whistling after him.

The whole neighborhood was aroused. He must get a break soon or capture was certain. The laces and long tongues of the negro's great shoes made him less fleet than usual. What a pass! Reduced to stealing a nigger's shoes. *There* was a dark hole. No! They'd look in such places first. The moment they turned the corner and found he had disappeared they would head straight for that hole. Keep running; keep running! One good thing—each corner was a respite from those damn' guns.

He cut across the street, his lungs bursting with the unusual exertion. He was running for his life now. Every inch that he widened the space between himself and his pursuers was an inch further from death. And he was gaining a little. If he could only get a break before they got the car after him.

Two bullets clicked the cement at his heels as he took another corner. This street was more brightly lighted. Two late-homing workmen plodded on the other side. A cab whizzed by. Man, there *was* a chance. If only an empty came along before those cops made the corner. He looked behind him. Headlights! But not a cab. A private car. It was all up. He must turn again at the next corner, and that would put him on a dull street where no cabs passed. God! how his lungs ached. Another burst of speed and he was around the corner before his pursuers had turned the one behind him. Now he had a chance. The private car turned the same corner and passed him, then slowed and drew toward the curb.

Zim's hand slid under his arm. If that was more cops he was going out shooting. They'd never send him up.

"Hey, buddy…. In a hurry?"

He had heard that voice—somewhere.

"Hop in."

Zim tried to see the speaker. The car contained four men.

"Who're you?" he muttered, slowing to a walk.

"We're angels, y' damn fool…. Pile in here b'fore those bulls get any closter, an' let go o' your rod."

This was talk he understood. Here were friends. The break! Zim sprawled into the back seat as the driver gave her the gas and the obedient car went like a rocket into the night.

CHAPTER THREE

No one spoke while Zim collected his body and settled to the business of catching his breath.

"Watch your feet," someone told him. "They's snakes in the bottom."

Zim only nodded and sat very still, wondering what he was in for now. As his heart quieted and he breathed more easily, he tried to see the faces about him. He could place them only vaguely. They were familiar—as fellow habitués of this resort or that. None of them were intimates. He started to lace his shoes.

"Come up!"

"My shoes."

"Nuts!"

"I gotta tie 'em."

"Lift 'em an' tie 'em…. Stay out o' the bottom o' this car!"

Zim crossed his legs alternately and laced and tied the enormous footgear.

"Them new shoes?"

"Huh! New to me."

"They look it."

"I stole 'em."

"No!"

There was a general laugh.

"You might 'a' done better at Thom McAn's."

"The store was closed."

They laughed louder.

"Shut up," said the man next to the driver. "This ain't no pic-nic party."

"Oh, hullo," said Zim. "I didn't recognize you, Mr...."

"That'll do.... Mister is plenty. Make up your mind where you want to get out o' this cab. We're goin' out of our way right now."

"Where are we?"

They told him.

"Just drop me anywhere. I'll be O.K. now. They were pressin' me pretty hard for a minute."

"If they hadn't been pressin' you we wouldn't never 'a' stopped."

"Well, thanks.... I'll do as much for you some time."

"Chris', I hope not."

"I'll get out wherever you say. But a good cab corner would do me better."

"We'll drop you at Westchester. Y' can get cabs there all the time."

"O.K."

A few more blocks and the car turned into a thoroughfare under an "L" trestle.

"Make sure there ain't none o' the 'finest' aroun' b'fore y' stop."

"Um," the chauffeur grunted and in a moment halted the car.

"So long, boys. Much obliged."

"So long."

The car pulled rapidly away.

Zim sighed deeply. That had been a break. They were good guys. Old Man Shields and his outfit—with a machine gun in the back seat! What the devil were they up to? Awful touchy about their artillery too. He chuckled. But it was white of them to stop. Now all he had to do was go into a convent or something and he was safe.

He hailed a passing cab and started to give his own address, then hesitated. The boss's? Not on your life. The garage? Schneider's?

"Times Square," he said. That would give him time to think. What should he do now? Staying away from his room was admitting guilt. Going there was courting disaster. Meeting any of the boys—or the boss—was dangerous to the outfit. The best thing to do was lay low and see what happened. Maybe they didn't know who he was or who he worked for. What a night! How many had he got? One, two—three or four anyway, and three wounded. He hadn't meant to do that. The boss had said to stay out of serious trouble. But what could he do?

At Columbus Circle he got out and walked to 5th Avenue. There he got in another cab and drove to 91st Street. Once more he walked a few blocks and took another cab to a small hotel on 6th Avenue. That ought to throw 'em off a little. Nobody actually knew what would work.

He registered as Henry Jackson and grinned as he remembered what had prompted the choice of that first name. "Poor Henry. He got quite a wallop." He paid for a week in advance and went to his room at once. He'd sleep a while, then get the early papers. How they would scream. Well, it was a hot racket. Sometimes you did and sometimes you didn't. It all depended. Sleep closed his weary eyes and he snored loudly.

CHAPTER FOUR

The boss clucked softly as the sound of a fusillade of shots came to him through the rumble of the big truck. "Zim's got himself in a jam," he said, speaking very loud to be heard above the noise of the truck. "I hope he makes it."

"Me too," said the laconic driver.

"Zim's a good boy."

"The best."

"I ought to go back an' give 'im a hand."

The chauffeur's feet changed position and the truck began to slow.

"Oh,—never mind. Go ahead a ways. No use everybody gettin' in on it."

The truck resumed its speed.

The boss had a name, but nobody ever used it. To his own men he was always "the boss", sometimes "The Boss!"—but never Clyde Poling. To the police he was just "Poling, the little rat", and his mother was long since dead.

"I'd hate to lose Zim."

"Yeah."

"They were pourin' a hell of a lot of lead."

"Yeah."

"I wonder if they got 'im."

"I wonder."

The boss had made up his mind. "Let me out."

"Yessir."

Poling dropped to the street before the truck could stop. "You'll be all right, now," he said as the chauffeur shifted gears. "Leave the wagon on 59th and the boys will pick it up. And get in bed inside of ten minutes after you leave the stuff. Things ain't right tonight."

"Yessir," the brief-spoken driver said, and the Mack rolled away like a barge into the night.

He walked through three or four blocks of slumbering houses to an all-night drug store, entered a phone booth and when the door was tightly shut gave a familiar number very softly. The sleepy girl did not understand and he gritted his teeth angrily. He repeated the call a little louder.

A receiver left a hook—somewhere—and a voice as low as his own spoke.

"Mel,—'s the boss."

"Yes, Boss."

"Zim got in bad."

"Um."

"Who's there?"

"Four 'f us."

"Got a can?"

"Sure."

"Look around. Zim might need you."

"Gotcha."

The receiver was replaced.

The little man held the hook down until he heard his coin drop, then he deposited another and called a different, unlisted number.

A very sleepy voice answered pettishly and thickly: "Hell—lo!"

"Let me speak to Happy."

"He's asleep."

"Let me speak to Happy."

That was the password—no other name, no other phrase, no other request would have had the slightest influence upon that sleepy voice. The august sleep of high officialdom is not interrupted except for very good friends, and only the very best friends of Deputy Commissioner Martin knew that phrase.

The majordomo shook his chief's shoulder timidly. It took the Commissioner several minutes to regain consciousness. It was a slow process. The servant knew the system perfectly and never tried to hurry it. He shook the shoulder lightly *twice*, then counted six. Shook the shoulder hard *once* and said, "Commissioner!" Then counted four. Then he punched the heavy chest four times, called loudly, and stepped back out of range of the flying fists. The man went through the ritual with half-opened eyes, leaped back and waited.

"Well," grunted the aroused police official. "Who is it and what does he want?"

"It's Poling, I think. And it's important."

Pudgy legs stuck out from the twisted bedclothes as he jerked the receiver from the extension.

"Hello."

"Hello, Happy. This is Poling."

"Yeah? How'd you make out?"

"You were right about the party. Everybody was there."

"But you made it?"

"Well, there was a lot of noise."

"The hell there was!"

"I left in such a hurry that I don't know exactly what happened."

"I gotcha."

"One friend of mine was still there when I left."

"Yeah."

"And I just wanted to give you this number—in case you see him in the morning."

"I gotcha."

"If you see him, mind; call B——6793…. O.K.?"

"O.K."

"G'night, Happy."

"G'night."

It was best to hide the real thing under a smoke screen of harmless words. So many branches of the law had stooped to tapping wires. Even the sacred private wires of Deputy Police Commissioners. Now, what else could he do?

He looked through the glass door into the half-lit drug store. No cops in sight. He left the store and soon hailed a passing cab. He'd better get out of the neighborhood. With the racket in its present precarious state he could not afford to be recognized near the scene of any fireworks.

"Times Square," he said to the driver. Like Zim, he figured the long ride would give him time to think.

If they had killed Zim, he had lost a valuable man. If they had taken him in, although Zim wouldn't talk, *he* would be called. And then everything would depend upon how serious Zim's crime was. There was nothing to do but wait until morning, stay away from the hang-out, away from his home, away from the barn. The stuff would be handled all right by the boys. He would go to the store, get his car, pick up Dolly or Pat and lay low in the apartment that even the police had not found *yet*. That was best. At 125th Street, Clyde signaled the cab to stop.

"Changed my mind." He paid the man and again used a public telephone. "I'll be by for you in forty minutes, sweetheart," he told Dolly Cushing. He walked two blocks to the plumbing establishment which flaunted his name from its window. He opened the wide garage door and drove his coupé out to the curb.

He locked up again and soon had entered the southbound river of traffic through Central Park. At a theatrical hotel he parked long enough to tell Dolly from the lobby that he was waiting for her, then he sat in the car until she came out.

She bubbled frothily across the walk, bumping into passers-by, and stuck her head through the door to say, "Hello, papak-ins," then she ran around and climbed in beside him.

"We're goin' to spend a damn' quiet evening, you and I…. Only two bottles of champagne, and then straight to bed. I have to get up early."

"Whatever you say, daddy. Gee, I seen the swellest squirrel dolman t'day."

CHAPTER FIVE

The four strange Samaritans drove rapidly away from the lighted street where they had dropped Zim.

"Who was that guy?" one asked. The fellow seated next to the driver answered without turning his butcher's neck. "Name's Zimbronski or somethin'. Call 'im Zim. Works for Poling."

"Oh, yeah? I heard o' him."

"Right guy."

"Yeah, me too. Pittsburgh or somewhere. Shoots too damn much."

The butcher's neck remained stationary, but its owner spoke again. "I wish t' God I had a few like 'im. Nobody ever accused you bastards of shootin' too much."

There was only silence in the car as it turned into upper Broadway. Three men were wondering why Jake Shields had aided in the escape of his chief rival's boldest gun hand.

They were old enemies—old friendly enemies—Poling and Shields. Their "business" paths often crossed, to no good purpose. Each had his mob. Each had his racket. Each was jealous of the other's prestige, power and publicity. Neither of them was a coward. They did not bar themselves away in luxurious cells and tell others what to do. Half of this mad game they played was in the active participation. Poling was in rum and gambling; Shields in dope and cash. Shields was in on the job tonight for both.

The tip had come straight to the Old Man and he was acting with characteristic promptness. In a Chinese laundry, it was said, there labored a young man who had just received a *barrel* of it. Even his boss wasn't wise. The kid was playing a lone hand. He was the only New York connection of a San Francisco outfit. The hop had been delivered that day. The money for the last previous batch would climb on a westbound train tomorrow. Tonight, and tonight only, both the hop and the cash were in the laundry—and the place stayed open practically all night.

The car slowed and stopped twenty feet away from the only lighted store in the block. The whole attack had been carefully planned. Every man knew his post. Everyone was ready—for anything. Five minutes before, a young woman had told the policeman on the beat that a man was trying to break into a window—three blocks away.

Lee Sin stopped ironing to grin into the barrel of a revolver. His palsied jaw stuttered some sing song phrases that paralyzed the other bare-armed Chinese workers.

"What want, gen'lemen?"

"Which one is Sam Kee?"

Lee Sin shrugged bravely. "No Sam Kee," he grinned. "No Sam Kee here."

"Quit lyin'! Who's Sam Kee—an' *quick!* We ain't got time to fool."

The proprietor was about to deny Sam Kee again when the gun belched and his grin was supplanted by a look of utter consternation. He bent a little at the knees and slid under the counter, clutching the record book of soiled shirts.

Shields turned to the second Oriental. "Now, *you!* Which one is Sam Kee?"

The man shook all over in an ague of fear. He pointed unsteadily to the last boy, at the rear of the room. "He—he—he Sam Kee."

"Go ahead," said Shields.

His tall accomplice rounded the counter and with a sharp knife already held in his left hand, slit the waistband of the white trousers Sam was wearing. A money belt with wads of bills and gold was around his hips. Slim cut that too, and—unable to hold gun, knife and belt with only two hands—dropped the knife and pocketed the money. Then, ramming the barrel of his pistol deep into the young Chinese' ribs, he said: "Now, where's the stuff?"

Sam did not move. The steel circle entered his flesh another quarter of an inch. "Only one more chance! Tell us—and we won't hurt you."

"Stuff downstairs."

"You're a dirty liar. C'mon, Chink. Cough up or you get this," jabbing once more with the gun.

Sam lifted his elbow and jerked his head to the right. "Stuff there." Behind a pile of clothes there peeped the corner of a paper suitcase.

Sweet Adeline, whistled, came through the door from the street. Slim grabbed the suit-case and ran. Shields covered his retreat, then backed out, whirled and entered the already moving car.

"That was close.... The harness is tryin' doors on his way down the block." Slim looked through the rear window. The excited Sam, holding his pants up with one hand, shook his other fist and yelled shrilly in Chinese. The officer, so easily beguiled from his beat a few minutes before, came running up to investigate the disturbance. The big car gained momentum with every fraction of a second.

CHAPTER SIX

A s the boss and Dolly sipped champagne, wrapped in each
other's arms, the program from WEAF was interrupted by
the telephone.

"Oh, hell!" said Dolly.

"Sh-h." Clyde picked it up. "Yes?"

"Mel talkin'."

"Yes, Mel." His voice was low and calm.

"We couldn't get within a mile o' the place, Boss. They got
the militia up there."

"What happened?"

"Why, seems like a man shot somebody."

"Yes?"

"Yeah. I circulated a bit on foot an' it seems three cops is
dead."

"Oh, that's too bad. Gangsters again, I suppose."

"I'm afraid so."

"Anybody else hurt? Not a cop, I mean."

"No. Seems the fellow that did it run away."

"And they don't know who it was?"

"Near as I could find out they ain't got the slightest notion
who done it—nor even why."

"Well, well."

"Yeah.... An' there's two wounded besides the three dead,
an'—"

"Not honest to God?"

"Uh huh. One was a Federal dick and the other one a fellow lives aroun' there. Not to mention a nigger with a busted haid."

"That's a record for a friend of mine to shoot at; eh, Mel? But it's too bad. There's too much trouble already."

"Y' want us t' keep on lookin' for Z—for—eh—Christmas?"

"No. Never mind. Go back to the place. There wasn't any slip about Mack?"

"No. He's all right. Those guys are all washed up."

"Well, suppose you just stay at the place in case you should hear from the wandering boy. Y' never can tell. He might need you later on."

"I gotcha…. An' say, Boss. We ran into the Kid…. Y' know?"

"What kid?" With so many double meanings flying about, Poling could not fathom the reference to the Kid.

"Chilton."

"Honest!"

"Yeah. He's plannin' a long trip."

"Nix."

"For his health."

"Where is he now?"

"Here."

"Where?"

"In the Bronx."

"Tell him I said it was O.K. to go see Pat, if he was sure he was alone."

"Yeah."

"Tell him she's at 338 Third Avenue," giving the address of the secret apartment.

"O.K."

"That all?"

"Yeah, I guess so."

"G'night … Get t' bed."

"Yeah, thanks."

Dolly looked at him seriously as he came back to the couch. "Is George back?"

"Yeah; can you imagine his nerve?"

"It'll lengthen Patsy's life."

"Let's call her. He'll be up here any minute."

Patsy Shelling was called and invited to join the party. When Clyde was through phoning, Dolly stroked his thin chin and shook her head slowly. "You ain't careful enough. You're takin' an awful chance, lettin' that guy come here. He's a crook. The police 're lookin' for him. It wouldn't do your plumbin' business any good to get mixed up with the police."

"That's true, Dolly. But isn't Patsy your friend?"

"Sure she is."

"Can they meet anywhere else?"

"No-o, I guess not."

"Well, then…. I guess I can take a chance."

"I hope they don't follow him."

"I hope not."

"He's a swell guy. Y' wouldn't think he could get in a jam like this."

"It's serious business. He'd get a long stretch if they caught him."

"They mustn't catch him. It would kill Pat."

Dolly's big eyes were swimming with unbidden tears. Her heart was heavy and her throat choky with love and sympathy. Poor Pat, poor Kid, poor daddy. She was sorry for all of them, sorriest for herself. Of middle class, midwestern birth, she had gravitated to New York and, like water, had found a level which seemed to be her own—that half world of not-very-good the-atrical people and not-very-bad crooks and tin-horn gamblers. There was nothing vicious in her, yet nothing strong or good.

She lacked the strength of character and the will so necessary to be either good or bad. Her morals were a patch-work of odds and ends, sewed together under the influence of splitting headaches on many "mornings-after". She did not know that Clyde Poling was the leader of a small army of unscrupulous criminals of all kinds. She thought he was a rather wealthy plumber who dabbled in bootlegging—as did half the men of her acquaintance. Had she suddenly come upon the knowledge of her lover's importance to the underside of the city's life, she would have done one of two things. The good in her would have caused her to renounce him, with bitter words about deceiving her, or—the ego of her, puny as it was—would have risen, swelling and stretching, to lord it over her girl friends as the mistress of a great and wicked killer.

But at this time Dolly had not discovered all the facts. She basked in Clyde's favor because he was tender and kind, always had plenty of money, the best drinks in town, a smooth-shaven and not ugly face, sharp, piercing eyes, and a figure unusually graceful. She was worrying now, about her good friend allowing so dangerous a character as George Chilton to come to this apartment. George was wanted by the police. He had killed a man. Young as he was, everyone knew he was bad.

What Dolly did not know was that George had committed the crime in Poling's employ. It had been a gambling quarrel, ending in a free-for-all with civilians and police. George was dealing stud. A sucker had squawked. He was a rich sucker, from out of town, unaccustomed to big-city ways. Through his drinks he had realized he was being trimmed, and had resented it. Though gray of poll and ready for bed two hours since, he had risen in his rage, overturned the card table and lunged at the Kid. The Kid, that is, George, had gone down under the sudden attack, among a dozen sticky glasses and several ginger ale bottles. The neck of one of those bottles had insinuated itself into George's palm and when he came up there was blood in his eye. The sucker was smashed mightily—right between the eyes. And the rage of the moment had raised and lowered the Kid's right arm five or six times before he could be stopped. The old giant from the sticks had been cut so badly that a doctor was called. That doctor had been considered safe. He would dress the wounds and keep his mouth shut. A hundred dollars or more for a ten-dollar call would seal his lips.

But the doctor had lost his nerve. As he worked over the old man he saw that the fellow might not live. It had been almost impossible to stay the flow of blood. A hospital was necessary. He left the gambling place and sought a policeman. To save himself he told the story and went virtuously to his home. Thirty minutes later the wagon had stopped before the door. A uniformed squadron had assailed the chained doors and George had been forced to shoot his way out. One policeman was dead and the lacerated pleasure seeker from out of town was in a hospital, hovering—wavering on the border line.

George had become a fugitive. That was a week ago. Now he was back. He was coming here. Dolly's sweetheart was allowing him to come here, just to see Patsy. Just because he was such a good fellow. It was dangerous. It might involve them all. Her spirits sank lower and lower, in spite of the wine and Clyde's kisses. She was afraid.

CHAPTER SEVEN

Old Man Shields and "Slim" lived together. "Slim" was from Texas. His name was Darby, John Darby, and any number of other things, depending upon the circumstances.

Shields had picked him up on the Bowery one night, panhandling for enough money to buy snow. He had taken him to his apartment, given him some of the precious powder, fed and clothed him. Later he learned that the fellow shot equally well with either hand. A fast friendship had grown between them. The heavy, brutal sarcasm of the Old Man had tickled Slim. He liked to hear him bawl out some henchman who had failed in a tight place. He was also very grateful for the assistance that had put him on his feet again. He was off the stuff, temporarily, although he handled quantities of it.

On the other hand, Shields admired any man who could hold his tongue and could shoot straight. Your eastern lead-pushers were none too accurate with their right hands. This Texan never missed—north or south.

They entered their home toward dawn, gratified and reassured that all was well by the whining growl of the great Belgian shepherd who stretched and yawned at their feet.

"Hello, Mutt. Anybody call?"

For answer the big animal reared and put two heavy paws on either side of Shields' thick neck, still yawning.

"Damn dog weighs more'n you do, Slim."

Darby laughed. "I guess he does." And patted the shaggy flank.

Without words, the two men hung up their clothes, divested themselves of holsters, cartridges and pistols. Slim gathered all of the tools of their wild trade, and after reloading the Old Man's, wrapped them all in an old newspaper, put the package in a galvanized iron garbage pail, dumped coffee grounds on top of the bundle and replaced the lid.

As they stood half nude, about to pile into bed, the telephone rang.

"Now, what the hell?"

"The boys!"

"Naw. They wouldn't."

"Trouble?"

"Not a chance."

"It's the good line." Meaning, the private telephone, not the one used for general calls and innocuous conversations.

"Yeah."

"They may have run into somebody before they could get away with the stuff."

"It was all fixed. Al could easy have caught that train."

"Well …"

Shields silenced the bell by lifting the receiver.

"Hello."

"Hello, fellah. This is Poling."

"Bad dreams to you."

"The same to you."

"What's on your mind?"

"I can't tell you on the phone, but I want to see you."

"I'm broke."

"So'm I. This is about a guy needs a vacation."

"Yeah?"

"He's a good sailor an' I thought maybe you needed one."

"It ain't the same bird I picked up in the Bronx, is it?"

"Who'd you pick up in the Bronx?"

"Well—a friend o' yours."

"Tonight?"

"Uh—huh."

"Honest? Is he all right?"

"I guess so. We lifted him out of a nasty hole."

"You're a square guy, fellah. I won't forget that."

"It ain't him, eh?"

"No, this is another one. Remember the Kid?"

"Oh, him?"

"Yeah."

"Well—I don't know why not. I'll see y' about it."

"When do you leave?"

"Tomorrow night."

"When can I see you?"

"Along in the afternoon.... But you'll have to fix it up with Happy."

"That won't be hard."

"Aw right. I'll see you."

"In Billy's."

"O.K."

"So long."

"So long."

Translated, the conversation had arranged for passage on a Cuba-bound freighter for one George Chilton, fugitive from justice, the final details to be arranged the following afternoon in a saloon on 53rd Street. The burden of police-fixing for this escape had been placed upon Poling's shoulders. Further, the temporary safety of Zim and the consequent obligation of the Boss to his rival had been established.

"Poling," the Old Man explained briefly to Slim. "He wants to get Chilton out o' the country. We're meetin' him in Billy's this afternoon."

"On the up-and-up?"

"We'll see."

The two men slept.

CHAPTER EIGHT

Poling turned from the phone to his guests. "There you are. All set. You sail for Cuba as an able-bodied seaman, about midnight tomorrow—that is, tonight…. If the cops don't get you between here an' the dock."

Patsy narrowed her eyes and almost whispered: "The cops will have orders to let him get on that boat…. I know my stuff."

"That ain't for me to say." Poling shrugged. "I can only go so far with Happy. Money ain't everything."

"What money ain't—I *am*," said Patsy bitterly. "The Kid's got to get away."

Chilton buried his haggard face in her lap. "Oh, God," he groaned. "I'd rather do a stretch."

"Cheer up, honey," the little, dark girl consoled him. "It ain't as bad as all that. I ain't forced to keep my promises, once you're on the boat. He's an old fat head, an' he's keen on this chorine. If we get you to Cuba, there ain't nobody gonna stop me from goin' there too…. I'll see you—in C-u-b-a."

The young man looked up, his eyes red with unshed tears and many sleepless nights. "You wouldn't go through with it, would you? You—you wouldn't go to him?"

She cradled his head in her arms. "You know I wouldn't."

"Let's have a drink," said the boss.

Dolly extended her empty glass toward the bottle. "You know more people," she said wanly.

"Yes," the boss laughed. "I know a lot o' people. They come in handy."

"Did you see the evening papers, Boss? They expect that guy to die." The young gambler's face showed the terrific strain of being hunted. His hair needed cutting. A stubble of glinting yellow bristles covered his chin. His shirt was dirty; his tie twisted; his suit much in need of brush and iron.

"Well, don't brag about it, son, and"—hardening—"don't call me 'Boss'. There's ladies present."

Dolly was feeling her drinks. The interchange had passed her by. But Patsy was more alert. Patsy had always been more alert than her room-mate. Her quick, dark eyes missed little that went on about her. She had always suspected Poling of being connected with her lover's delinquency. The transactions of this evening were strengthening her conviction. This dapper little money-man was no plumber. Good fellow that he obviously was, there was something sinister in his quiet calmness, some indication of untold reserve power in his easy-going ways. *Boss*, was he? Damn him! But she said nothing. Her bosom rose and fell quickly under the pleasing restraint of a knitted silk dress. Poling's eyes lingered over her short, perfectly carved figure. Dolly was less compact, given more to roving lines and less confined areas. No wonder Happy wanted Pat. Who wouldn't? And with Chilton out of the way—who could tell? He'd probably get Happy sore at him if he made the play, but there were many ways—and devious.

He saw her looking at him sharply, the light casting violet shadows under her lashes, her small jaw tightly set.

"What's the matter, Pat? ... Y' look as if you'd like to eat me."

She recovered her presence of mind. You had to be careful. You couldn't be too careful around these racketeers, these oily friends, these killing, hard-boiled, polite gunmen. George wasn't one of them. He was a kid gone bad. Look at him now, clinging to her shoulders, almost ready to cry after his first big offense. His hair was soft and wavy, his mouth unhardened. This little man, staring at her breasts and grinning, was all hay-wire, ruthless, experienced, deadly. She had to be careful. Even if he was responsible for George's crime, he was also the only means of his salvation. Her appeal to Happy was worthless without this man's aid. She relaxed quickly, darted a glance at Dolly, then smiled and winked meaningly at Clyde. She would play both of them. She would make this *Boss* think she desired him. She would make any kind of a contract with the crooked Commissioner. She would do anything to get George safely away. She squeezed Chilton's hand as if to apologize for her perfidy, as if to tell him she did not mean it and that she was doing it all for him.

Chilton became more natural under the influence of the banter and chaff that filled the kitchen as the girls prepared breakfast. The odor of coffee and the smiles of these friends gave him new courage. Here was his sweetheart, standing by him. Here was the Boss himself, taking a big chance to get him away—safe from the chair. His escape seemed assured. After nearly a week of fear and hiding, he was going to be able to call his soul his own. He sent up a little prayer to the God his parents had given him—so few and yet so many years ago. If he got out of this mess, he would go straight—always. He'd get a job in Havana. He'd make his pile honestly. He'd come back and marry Patsy. If he only got out of *this*.

And as these four drank coffee as preparation for sleep, two husky fellows stowed the last cases from the bowels of the capacious Mack truck in "the barn", well concealed from the law, and Al Turner, of Shields' brood, left the Pennsylvania Station in Washington, D. C., carrying a paper suit-case full of dope.

CHAPTER NINE

Zim spread the morning papers on his bed and lit a cigarette. Whew! What a night! The reporters sure had had their hands full. Look at this.

CRIME WAVE GRIPS CITY

Four Dead, Three Injured
Gangland's Toll Between Suns

UNDERWORLD ANSWERS POLICE

AFTER SHAKE-UP TO END CRIME

The wholesale transfer and readjustment of the city's police department announced yesterday as an offensive against organized crime has been ineffectual. As if to flaunt their immunity in the face of law and order, gunmen and gangsters killed four men, wounded a fifth and injured two others in one of the bloodiest nights of crime in the last twenty years. Three of the slain as well as the one wounded were police officers. The other man killed in cold blood was Lee Sin, proprietor of a Chinese laundry,——Broadway. No arrests have been made. The guilty gangs in the two separate sallies escaped unscathed.

"Two, eh?" Zim shook his head. "So those birds bumped off a Chink.... To hear these papers you'd think I was an army."

> The dead were: —— —— —— ——
> The wounded were: —— —— ——
>
> An ambush to intercept a truckload of alcohol and rare wines was attacked from the rear by a party of the rum runner's friends, evidently warned by some "higher-up" in police circles. As the party of federal officers, under the leadership of——, were about to stop the speeding truck, firing broke out behind them, drawing their attention and killing...
>
> It was impossible to determine the exact number in the gang...

That was good. Saving their faces. The dogs. They wouldn't admit that one lone man had done so much damage and then escaped on foot.

> The owner of the truck is known and it is said by both city and state officials as well as by——, in charge of Prohibition Enforcement, that he would be questioned today.
>
> The only clew to the identity of any of the murderers was a pair of shoes...

"Haven't they found my hat? ... They must not of looked good."

There followed a highly colored and greatly exaggerated account of the battle. The "tipster" was to be found and ousted. The peace was to be maintained at all costs.

In another column Zim read the details of his erstwhile friends' raid. There, also, was a clew. A long sharp knife. The loss at the laundry was described as the "life-savings of a young Chinese who intended to return to his sweetheart in China". Sam Kee had preferred not to mention the paper suit-case full of opium.

Various papers had taken different leads. Some referred to the fracas in the gambling den only a week before and the fact that there was still another murderer at large. Editorials screamed for arrests. The reign of the Kings of Crime must end!

Zim read every word of it, highly excited. His self-esteem rose as he and his kind were referred to as heinous, unscrupulous, dastards, doing their dreadful work in the slimy shadow of some legal cloak. Then he went out and bought a cap—and further along the same street a new pair of shoes. He debated about leaving the old ones and decided to take them along. He looked furtively at the traffic officers he passed. They were all busy with their whistle blowing. He wasn't well known to the traffic squad anyway. It would be a long time before they got around to him. And by that time Happy and the Boss would have it all fixed up. He just had to watch his step with the iron. A taxi accident or an inquisitive maid at the hotel might show his gun. Then trouble.

He took a subway to Canal Street and left the negro's shoes in a trash barrel, then drove back to the Western Union office near Times Square in a cab. Two plainclothes men stood at the curb. "Go ahead," he told the driver. "Forty-seventh and Broadway." That was close. He'd better stay inside. He risked a phone call to the boss.

"I can't tell you what I think of you over the phone, you damn fool. But when I see you—God help you."

"Why, Boss—"

"Never mind! I'm gonna take that thing away from you. Children ain't allowed to play with matches."

"I was only—"

"You were only tearin' down the Paramount Building with *me* in the basement,—you half-wit."

"I thought—"

"Not in your whole life, you never thought. You only thought you thought. Now listen. Bring that Roman candle of yours an' be at Hans Schneider's back door at eleven tonight. That's all. G'by."

Zim slammed out of the phone booth, almost blind with rage. That was the thanks he got for slaughtering half the police force. That was the kind of an ungrateful so-and-so *he* was working for. Take it away from him, huh? Roman candle was it?! He'd shove that Roman candle down his throat! Half-wit, eh? He stumbled down the street muttering to himself, bumping into people, cursing and jerking his head. That's the way it always was. The big money guy never did nothin'. Just sat on his fanny and grabbed and grabbed and grabbed, while honest strong-arms like him went out an' did all the dirty work—and burned for it in the end.

He climbed the steps to a saloon and grew still more angry at the delay of the doorman. Silly damn' fool, peekin' through a slot. As if they wouldn't let anybody in if he had money to spend.

By eight o'clock he was very drunk and he hated Clyde Poling as fiercely as he had loved him the night before. "Bawl me out, will he? I'll show 'im."

CHAPTER TEN

A narrow, bricked passage-way led from 86th Street to the side door of Schneider's. Inside that door one had a choice of paths. One could enter the kitchen of the restaurant by another door, on the street level, or one could ascend a short stairway, turn on a landing and reach the second floor. There, again, one had an alternative. There was a door admitting one to a bare and windowless room, or there were more steps, leading to Schneider's own apartments above.

Mel, he of the telephone voice who had assembled three fellows and started out to look for Zim after the shooting, chose to enter the windowless room. Mel was an old hand, an old head. Bert Melcher—"Mel" from coast to coast wherever an old hand was welcome. His hair was gray, his mustache almost white. He wore glasses, but got along very well without them if need arose.

He grunted at the sudden blackness of the interior when he opened the door. He was the first arrival. His hand found the familiar switch and flooded the barren room with light from a ceiling fixture. There were two enormous round tables, poker tables from the back room of an old saloon, with racks around the edges for chips. A dozen chairs, half of them broken, and a week-old newspaper completed the room's furnishings.

Besides the one door through which the man entered, there were two others, each leading to another room.

Mel pressed a push button set in the wall and entered each of the other rooms in turn, lighting them and then turning the lights off when he was satisfied that they were empty. He drew up a chair facing the stair door and sat down to read a paper he carried. As the waiter mounted the steps the old man loosened his coat—in case it wasn't a waiter.

"Beer," he said, going back to his paper, "and pretzels."

"*Yah. Ein seidel!*"

Mel nodded and continued to read.

> Thomas L. Brown, wealthy contractor from Flint, Michigan, succumbed today at Mt. S——Hospital after a valiant fight for life. Death was attributed to wounds received in a gambling house brawl. George Chilton, a character known to the police, is still at large although every effort has been made to capture him. Chilton, it is alleged, is also wanted for the murder of Detective Gilray, the same evening. He is said to be a member of a very powerful gang of thieves and blackmailers...

Mel's beer was delivered. "Thieves and blackmailers! Ain't that a break? I should live all these years to be called a blackmailer. Oh, well—" he drank deeply.

The waiter backed into the room. "Two gentlemen," he whispered. "Do you know them?"

Mel rose and looked over the man's shoulder. "Yeah, they're all right…. C'mon up, boys."

It was Shields and Slim Darby.

"Hello, Mr. Shields. Hello, Two-gun, how's the long-horn?"

"O.K., Mel, how's the ranger?"

"Smart…. Smart enough to get out o' the rangers."

The three laughed. "We early?"

"A little. They'll all be driftin' in. What time does your tub sail?"

"They wait for Al. He comes back with cash."

"Not meanin' to pry."

"Oh, no offense…. I never carry all my eggs in one basket. Al brings the cash back. I bank some an' send some away. Ten or twenty dollars profit," Shields winked broadly. "It's nothin' to brag about."

"Petty larceny, eh?"

"Yeah, that's it. Petty larceny." His neck got very red as he laughed at the crude joke.

"Tell the waiter what you'll drink, gents. I'll guarantee the quality."

The newcomers ordered and the waiter went down the steps.

"How's tricks?" asked Shields, sitting down at the table.

"Not so good," Mel answered. "Brown is dead. That means two skulls on the Kid."

Slim was investigating the two doors.

"Yeah, I read it."

"Tough."

"Yeah. Say—that Zimmy of yours raised hell, didn he?"

"Wait'll the boss gets 'im. Whew, he's sore."

"Sore! Say, I'll hire that boy. He ain't afraid o' nothin'."

Poling stepped into the room, unheard. "I wish he was afraid o' somethin'. This damn killin's got to stop."

"Hello, Poling. What do you care? They ain't got nothin' on you."

"You ought to muzzle that gat o' yours too, Shields. It ain't gonna do any of us no good to go aroun' cuttin' down cops and Chink laundry men."

"Who says I cut down a Chink?" Shields left his chair, belligerently.

"Keep your shirt on. I ain't got a picture o' the deed, but you know who did it. And what's more, you know it's damn' foolishness."

"Say, am I here to do you a favor or ain't I? Your little boys go aroun' gettin' into trouble an' y' come to me to get 'em out—an' then you bawl me out for cuttin' down a damn Chink. Who the hell do you think you are?"

"I'm not bawlin' you out. I'm just askin' you if you think it makes things any easier?"

"I don' know nothin' about that Chink."

"All right, all right. If you take that attitude, I don't know anything about these bulls."

Shields wagged his head. "O' course not. *You* don't. But remember that if it wasn't for me Zim'd be in Bridewell *now*."

"Jus' wait'll I get that little quick-trigger bird. I bet I teach him."

The waiter made another trip for drinks. While he was gone the bad blood increased. Mel and Slim said little. They had known each other on the Mexican border, many years before. They did not understand these eastern thugs very well. They kept out of it. But there was more at stake than "the point" of an argument as these two wrangled. They liked to think of themselves as rival Kings, leaders of men, and their discussions might lead to open declarations of war.

Tonight, Poling was taking more than he would have done under ordinary circumstances. He wanted to get Chilton on the high seas. Then he'd show them all where to get off. He had not the slightest doubt that Patsy would become the mistress of Happy—the "higher-up"—and he trusted himself to win Patsy. Then, with that strangle hold on the law, with all his money and his loyal pack, there wouldn't be room enough in any city for Old Man Shields and himself. Shields would have to go.

Chilton stumbled climbing the steps, and almost at his heels, came Zim, howling drunk.

"Sit down, Kid. I want to talk to this num-skull," Poling directed. But Zim had recognized Shields and surprise had driven vengeance from his mind. He lunged across the room and grasped the thick hand of his savior of the evening before.

"Boy, oh, boy. Here's a boy. Here's a boy! Boss, mitt the boy. There's a boy. Whoopee. He pick' me up. He stop's car t' pick m' up. Boy, oh, boy. Whoopee."

"Give me your gun, Zim." Poling extended his hand.

"Yeah. An' you not even grateful. I go get th' 'ole p'lice force an' get m' head blowed off an' y' say's a Roman candle. By God. I'll give it to you. I'll give it to you in the throat!" The drunken gunman drew his automatic and pointed it at Clyde's head. Like a half-back punting, Clyde's toe rose swiftly in a vicious kick, sending the gun spinning toward the ceiling, at the same time a left caught the fellow beside the ear. When he looked up from the floor Poling had him covered. "No man ever pulled a rod on me an' lived, you little—ant. You're goin' for a ride."

The whole turn of the tables had consumed no more than three seconds. It was for such lightning decisions, such amazing speed of mind and body that every follower of the Boss respected him. While his foot kicked, his left fist smote and his right hand drew from a hip holster.

The room was perfectly still. "Get up an' sit down like a man."

Zim licked his lips, burning with inner fumes of alcohol. "I'm drunk, Boss…. I'm sorry."

Someone had put Zim's automatic on the table.

"Sit down…. Now, what's next?"

Chilton spoke: "I just left Patsy, Boss. She's seen Happy. Nobody'll stop me an' Mr. Shields' man—"

"Who's that?" Clyde asked, turning to his rival.

"That's Al. He ain't here yet."

"Go ahead."

"That's all. The rest is up to Mr. Shields."

"O.K.... Al will be here any minute. You two ride to the Brooklyn Bridge in a cab. Then you walk. Al knows where the ship is. They're all clear an' steam is up. Tugs are fast. She'll leave the minute you two step aboard."

"An' she don't dock 'til Havana?"

"Right."

"Good. Push 'at button an' we'll have a drink.... Put this back, Zim." Poling pushed the automatic toward the crestfallen gladiator. "The ride is off. But don't ever argue with me." He rose and turned his back deliberately to the entire group.

Mel, not so foolhardy in trusting a drunken man, slipped his own gun into his lap and watched Zim carefully as he slowly slid the thing back under his coat. The Boss had won several victories, hands down. Shields was impressed.

As they drank and talked, waiting for Al to return from Washington, Poling's restless fingers encountered a deck of cards on the ledge under the table top. He riffled them, between drinks; sorted out three aces and tossed them again and again with rapid, skillful fingers. The entire party was nervous and ill at ease. Their conversation was brittle and unsustained. Not one of these men had anything to say to any of the others. Friendly and amiable as they seemed, superficially, they distrusted each other, and each new cigarette only thickened the atmosphere already dense.

"Ain't they no way to get a little air in here?" Slim asked.

"No," said Poling. "The only air is outside.... Did you fellows ever see this trick?" He performed a simple sleight-of-hand feat which reminded Mel of one. The deck was passed and he performed it, without breaking the tension that seemed every moment to increase.

The waiter brought more drinks and closed the door behind him. "I know a good one," said Chilton, rousing from his lethargy. "Split the deck in three piles and I'll go out o' the room. Anybody can touch one o' the piles, and when you're ready, I'll come back in an' tell y' which one was touched."

"On'y your youth saves you, Kid," Slim drawled. "We cut our teeth on that one."

"I learned one from a Hindu once," said Poling. "Let's see how that goes.... There's five of you.... You each take ten cards an' go out o' the room. That leaves me with two cards.... Everybody tears up one card—oh, it raises hell with the deck—and puts the pieces in his pocket, or anywhere. Y' come back, an' somebody shuffles 'em—with my two back in the pack. Then you deal me seven off the top and I'll name the five torn cards for a thousand bucks a card."

Shields raised his brows and pursed his lips. "Always bettin' on something."

Chilton said: "*We* shuffle?"

"Yes."

"And you only see seven cards?"

"That's it."

"You're crazy."

"I'll do it—for a thousand bucks a card. You can pool on me if you like."

"A Hindu trick?"

"Yeah. It's mind readin'."

They laughed nervously.

"Let's go," said Shields. "I'll fade the first two."

Clyde took two cards at random from the pack. "Shuffle the rest."

The waiter entered and whispered hoarsely to the Boss. "There's a girl downstairs, says she has to see you." Patsy had followed the man in. Slim arose and removed his hat. Chilton's chair banged to the floor as he ran to her side. "What's up?"

"Happy's double-crossin' us. I came as fast as I could to tell you. He was all right until Brown died, now he's welching. The Mayor and the chief commish have just left his office. They ask' for his resignation. Don't stop me. I know what I'm talkin' about. It's the election an' the damn newspapers. Happy has to show some pinches in twenty-four hours or quit an' get out. He ain't gonna get out. He's gonna pinch you when you start to get on that boat."

"Happy wouldn't do that," Poling interjected. "He'll let him go."

"Happy's gonna do that. I know it. I just left his ante-room. I heard the whole thing. The only way to beat him is to go down there as quick as you can, alone. They think two men are comin'. They know about Al. They won't bother you if you're alone—they won't even be there if you hurry."

"What'll I do, Boss?"

"Y' sure it's all straight, Patsy? No hysterics?"

"No, no, no. I'm *telling* you."

"Run for it, Kid. I knew somethin' like this'd happen," Poling glared at Zim.

"Now, wait a minute," said Shields. "Suppose your Kid gets away. Who's Happy gonna pinch then—huh?"

"What difference does it make?" Patsy screamed at him. "C'mon, Kid."

"It makes a hell of a lot of difference to me," said Shields. But Patsy and George were gone. The door at the foot of the stairs opened and closed behind them.

Poling stood very still turning the two cards over and over in his hands. "They'll never make it," he said at last. "If Happy don't want the Kid to go—they'll never make it."

"Aw, it's all your fault," Shields growled. "Butcherin' half the town—"

"Listen, big boy," said Zim. "Y' gave me a lift las' night and I thanked y' for it. But if you don't let up on me, I ain't above pastin' you now."

"Shut up, Zim," said the Boss. "Let go your iron, there, Openspaces. I'm doin' a card trick."

The waiter wiped the table, took their order, and left with his rattling tray.

"Save your card trick 'til we get this settled.... How's that boy gonna find the ship without Al?"

"If Happy knows where it is—so does Patsy."

"Who is this jane?"

"She's gone on the Kid, but she's been playin' Happy so's he'd let him go."

"Cripes, I hope they don't take Al; he's filthy with money."

"Yeah? ... Maybe it's marked."

"Naw, he's bringin' it from—out o' town."

"I see."

The waiter appeared with their drinks.

Shields rose and paced the floor. "By God, if they take Al tonight I'll get you, Poling. I'll drive every mother's son of your gang into the Hudson."

Clyde made a mocking face. "Sorry, old man—we don't drive so easy."

Mel turned to Slim. "Your boss says the damndest things."

There was a knock at the door. Five hands gripped pistol butts. "Come in."

Al entered and quickly shut the door behind him. "Does Happy know about this dive?" he asked before anyone else could speak.

"No," said Clyde. "But he'd like to."

"That's good. They met my train. I saw 'em, naturally. I ducked. They followed me. I been runnin' all over town to shake 'em. My God, they're everywhere. I never seen so many bulls in my life. That's why I'm late."

"Y' sure they didn't follow you here?"

"Nope. I doubled back on First Avenue and took a cab across town. What's up anyway? They act like there'd been a murder."

"That ain't funny," Zim hissed.

"Well, …" Al looked to his chief in embarrassment.

"It's all right," said Shields. "Let's have it."

Al pitched a fat wallet on the table. Shields' eyes lit in miserly anticipation. "Now, I'll play you that trick for *five* thousand a card," he said.

"Done," said Clyde. "Five thousand it is."

"You're crazy, Boss," said Mel. "Nobody can do that."

"We ain't got time anyway," said Shields, regretting his rashness.

"You said *five.* I took you. Don't welsh, Jake. The longer this boy waits the better his chances of making the boat."

"All right," Shields said grudgingly. "What do we do?"

"You each take ten cards and go out of the room…. You too, Al. Take ten cards…. You can step out at the head of the steps, Jake. Al and Zim can go in there"—indicating one of the two doors—"and Mel and Slim in there"—nodding to the third door. "Each of you tears up a card and hides the pieces—in your pockets—anywhere. Then, when I call you, you all come back."

The five men left the room, each carrying ten cards. Three doors clicked shut. The Boss was alone in the smoke-filled room. He tossed his two cards on the table and rose as if for a seventh-inning stretch. He lifted his arms high over his head and yawned. Then a large caliber automatic rattled behind him. Splintering wood. A scuffle of feet. He turned, groping back of him for his own gun. Then, as the doors opened and the men came rushing back, the Boss settled to the floor in a pool of his own blood. A sickening sound came from his throat, like gas. He tried to rise; his gun was in his hand, as yet unfired. He settled back to the floor, his sharp, bright eyes dimmed by death.

PART TWO

CHAPTER ELEVEN

M el, the old hand, the ex-ranger and long-time pal of the Boss, leaned over the body. "Some filthy swine," he said coldly. "He's got it in the back."

Several pairs of feet pounded up the steps. Like a panther, the gray-haired man leaped to the door and stepped out. The waiter and Schneider headed the procession of cooks and bus boys.

"Go on down stairs," he said sharply. "And keep everybody off these steps."

"*Mein Gott*, Mr. Melcher, iss it something? Is somebody hurt? Now comes the police.... Oh, *mein Gott!*"

"Back in the store, Heinie. An' keep your mouths shut!" Then he reëntered the room. Zim, Slim and Al stood like statues, regarding the corpse at their feet. Flight had not yet occurred to them; their minds were fogged from bad air, smoke and drink. They were stunned by the most unexpected of all unbelievable events. *The Boss* was dead! Somebody had shot the Boss.

"Let's see your gun, Zim," said Mel calmly.

No one moved. Zim turned slowly toward the taller, older man with eyes which scarcely saw what was before them. "Huh?"

"Let me see your gun." He extended his hand.

Then the fighting Zim came back to earth. "The hell I will. It ain't been out. It's full. This Al was with me.... Why, damn you, are you meanin' *I* did this?" Then the picture of his quarrel with the Boss earlier in the evening came back upon him with a rush. "My God," he said, "it sure looks bad for me; don't it?" He looked from one to another of the group. Then he missed one face. "Where's Old Man Shields?" he cried. They looked at each other, then around the room. Shields was the only one missing.

Mel ran back to the door. "Look at this!" One panel of the door at the head of the steps had been riddled with bullets. Splinters stuck out in the room. The shots that had killed Clyde Poling had been fired from beyond that door—and Old Man Shields had been out there alone.

Mel opened the door. On the landing were ten playing cards, and at the foot of the first step leading to the apartment above lay a heavy automatic. The three men watched him pick it up and slip it in his pocket.

"Come on," he said. "I'm going *up.*"

Grimly, silently, slowly, those four ascended the steps, guns in hand. Mrs. Schneider opened the door only a crack at their summons. "No, gentlemen. No one has came here. Oh, such trouble. Iss my man all right?"

"Yes," said Mel. "He's all right."

"Listen," said Zim. "What's that?" At the street door below, voices were arguing heatedly.

"It's cops," said Al. "They're everywhere."

"Let us in, Mrs. Schneider." As they closed and locked the door behind them—"Is there a way to the roof?"

"In the kitchen." She led the way.

"I feel like a dog, desertin' the Boss," said Zim. "But God knows *I* can't stand no police parades after las' night."

"Wait a minute," said Mel thoughtfully. "They can't pin anything on me.... I guess I'll go back."

"Better not, Mel," Slim advised. "It'll be a terrible mess—an' y' can't do Poling no good."

Nodding assent, Mel followed the others up the narrow stairs and through the trap door to the roof of the three-story building.

Zim looked back through the rectangle of light and whispered hoarsely. "You haven't seen anyone, Mrs. Schneider. Understand? You didn't see us."

The German woman waved her hand in token of comprehension and they replaced the trap door.

"Now," Al growled, "where the hell do we go from here?"

Five connecting buildings stretched to their left, all the same height. The roofs were separated only by brick fences, not over three or four feet high.

"We better separate," said Mel. "We stand a better chance. And mum's the word, until we see the papers. Is that O.K.? ... Not a word about Shields until we see the papers."

"Nobody knows he did it," said Slim testily. "All you've got is his gun. Suppose you give it to me."

"No you don't, big boy. I'll tote that cannon right along with me. I may need it."

"You two can scrap as long as you like," said Zim. "I'm gettin' out o' here." And he ran swiftly across the dark roofs to a fire escape half-way down the block.

"The Old Man's gat ain't gonna do you no good, Slim. Let this guy keep it. C'mon, I'm gonna try to make the boat." Al started away.

"Don't be a sap," Slim spat. "They'll blow up the harbor to stop that boat after *this.*"

"They'll blow up nothin'. So long." And Al vaulted one low brick wall.

"Let's not fight, Texas.... I won't give this gun in unless it's necessary. You can trust me. Let's get out o' this?"

Slim looked at his old friend a long time. "I don' know, boy. Once a ranger, always a ranger. I ain't above doubtin' you—in the clinches."

There had been no outcry from either of the descending men. Apparently they had not been detected. The two tall men shook hands. "So long." Slim chose the nearest iron ladder, Mel moved cautiously toward the one chosen by Zim. Two hundred feet from the manhole through which they had climbed, he stopped, lay down on his belly and peered cautiously over the roof's edge to the street below.

A crowd surrounded the doorway and five uniformed officers moved back and forth, urging all to move on. Mel recognized one heavy detective who seemed to be in charge. "McQuirk, eh? He's never seen me in specs. If I can get around there, maybe I can get an earful." Cautiously he let himself down on to a porch roof, then to its bannister and the rear, outside stairway of a house. "Heaven will protect the working girl," he muttered and picked his footing carefully through a basement areaway. His advance was unchallenged, and he gained the street as fresh groups raced past toward the jangling patrol wagon, just coming to a halt. He followed them, hurrying a little as if out of curiosity.

There was little to see or hear. The cops tried without success to keep the growing crowd moving. They were guarding the doors of Schneider's cabaret. No one was allowed to leave. An ambulance clanged up behind the patrol and several very self-conscious, white-coated attendants worked their way through the crowd. Almost immediately, the private car of a medical examiner stopped and a little Jewish doctor bustled officiously into the passageway.

"What happened, neighbor?" Mel asked the man next to him.

"Them gangsters," the fellow informed him, "have killed ten people."

"You don't say!"

"Yeah, it's gettin' terrible. A man ain't safe nowhere."

Someone slid an arm into Mel's. Without turning, the old man pointed the automatic in his pocket at the stomach of the man and waited. "What'll you take for the story?" a voice whispered in his ear. "The whole story. Just like it happened."

Mel didn't turn so much as his eyes even then. A reporter, likely, someone who knew him. Funny how he instinctively got the drop on a fellow that way. The gun was probably empty. It was Shields' gun. The lead was all in the Boss, on the floor upstairs. What wouldn't this fellow give to know that the gun that killed Clyde Poling was at that moment pointing at his own middle.

"Don't never take a man's arm like that, son. Not ever." Then he turned around. It was a reporter, as he had thought. A bright young fellow with a memory for faces.

"The *Gazette* will pay you five grand for the story, and not mention your name."

"Do you feel this?"

There was no mistaking the meaning pressure.

"You wouldn't do that just because I make you a business proposition."

"I'd do that damn quick if I saw a flash-light go off right now."

"I haven't got a photographer with me. You overestimate the speed of the press.... What do you say? Five grand—and no names named."

"I say, 'get the hell out of here,'—an' *don't* go towards McQuirk."

"O.K., buddy. I ain't arguin' with *you*." The reporter moved away. But the conversation had attracted attention. His neighbors looked at Mel quizzically, and as he moved away two men followed him. He engaged a cab at the edge of the crowd. "Times Square," he said, without thinking. "And hurry."

"Yes, sir."

The reporter watched him go, then sought McQuirk. "Bert Melcher just left here in a cab, Mac. I just thought you might like to know."

"Why didn't you tell me before?"

"I didn't see him before."

"Aw, bunk.... Hey, Tom. Go get Bert Melcher. He just left here in a cab." A detective obediently left the crowd and entered a taxi. "Times Square," he said with rare prescience. "And hurry."

CHAPTER TWELVE

M cQuirk came into the crowded room from the street, a burly assistant on each side of him. "Lord," he coughed, "everybody quit smokin' … It's too hot in here." A chair was vacated for him and the medical examiner rose from his crouch beside the body and held out a bundle of letters and papers taken from the pocket of the dead man.

"There's the rest," he said, pointing to the table. "I'll have to pry his gun out of his hand. He's frozen to it."

"Never mind now," said McQuirk. "I want to get rid of this gang as quick as I can.… Who owns this place?" A policeman pushed Schneider forward. McQuirk yawned viciously and ran his giant hand over his heavy-featured face. "Wurroff," he growled. "Ain't there no way to get air in here?"

Schneider trembled before the majesty of this colossus who could complain about ventilation in the presence of violent death. He licked his trembling lips and tried to make words form in his parched throat.

"You the landlord?"

"Grrss a her."

"What!?"

"Yes, sir."

"That's better … What's your name?"

"Schneider."

"You own the cabaret downstairs?"

"Yes, sir."

"Sell booze?"

"No, sir."

McQuick waved his hand in tired resignation. It was a lie he had expected. Why waste time asking fool questions like that? "You know who this man is?"

"Aw—no, sir."

"Sure?"

"Yes, sir."

"Who is he?"

"I don' know."

"Know who killed him?"

"No, sir."

"How's he happen to be here?"

"He ask' me if he could."

"*He* asked you?"

"Yes, sir.… He come in with four or five men an' says they want t' be alone. I says, here's this room. They ordered supper an' then I heard shots."

"Supper, huh?" McQuirk pushed a beer stein and a whisky glass an inch or two across the dirty table in ironic punctuation of his question. "What do you serve in these—corn-beef an' cabbage?"

"I dunno." Schneider shrugged phlegmatic German shoulders. Maybe he better play dumb. The more stupid he seemed, the less prying the questions would be.

"Ever see any of the other men before?"

"No, sir. They were all strangers."

"How many of 'em?"

"Four—five."

"Six?"

"Maybe. I didn't pay much attention. There was quite a lot of them."

"Who brought 'em their 'supper'?"

Schneider indicated the sullen-eyed waiter who had been listening belligerently.

A late-coming reporter squeezed through the crowd at the door. "Hello," he nodded. "Who is it?"

"It's Boss Poling," a policeman told him. "Why don't you read the papers?"

"Poling! My God, who got him?" The scribe was too shocked at the magnitude of the story to resent the jibe at his tardiness.

"That's what this party's for … t' find out."

"You don't tell me."

"Shut up," said McQuirk, then turned again to the waiter. "What's your name?"

"Eddy Haas."

"Yeah—well, Eddy, did you know any o' these seven men?"

"No, sir."

"Any of the *eight?*" the question had been shot at him with bullet-like speed.

"There was only seven."

"Seven, eh? Countin' him?" indicating Poling.

"Yes, sir."

"Where's the other six?"

"I don' know."

"Did they pay their check?"

"No, sir."

"How much was it?"

"I don' know."

McQuirk raised his brows in mock surprise. "Seven suppers in a private room an' you don't know what the check was? … Let's see it."

"I ain't got it."

"Where is it?"

"I—I lost it."

"You got a good waiter there, Snider. He'll make money for you. Come on, now; cut the comedy, you birds. There ain't no check because it didn't matter how much these guys drank. They supply you with your liquor an' you know they'll drop off an extra case or two the next day to more than make up for a party. There was seven men instead o' four and you know every damn one of them by name. Now, who were they? Quick! Or by God you'll sleep in jail."

Schneider and his waiter looked at each other in stunned amazement. No unpaid check in their combined experience had wrought such havoc. McQuirk stood up. "Come on, who was here? They all been here before. There was Poling, Bert Melcher ... who else? ... Take this down, Harry."

The two Germans remained silent. This man was a wizard. He had found out so much so quickly. Where would he stop? Every time he spoke he uttered a new truth which he could not know—but did.

"Lock 'em up," he ordered. "We ain't got time to fool around.... Who're you?"

"Firs' cook."

"What'd these seven men eat?"

Schneider, being pulled none too gently out the door, cast one despairing glance at his first cook and was jerked away.

"I don' know."

"Did you make up seven orders for this room?"

"No, sir. They were drinkin'."

"O.K.... You didn't see them yourself, did you?"

"No, sir. I been in the kitchen."

"O.K. J' hear the shots?"

"Yes, sir."

"What'd it sound like?"

"Like—like shots."

"I mean, how many did you hear?"

"They came so fast I couldn't count 'em. They all ran together, almost like one shot."

"Yeah? Too fast for you, huh? Did y' ever hear an automatic go off?"

"No, sir."

"O.K…. What'd y' do when y' heard the shots?"

"I ran out."

"Where?"

"Downstairs."

"See anybody?"

"No, sir."

"Y' didn't answer that too quick! Who'd y' see?"

"I didn't see anybody."

"Who else ran out when you did?"

"Mr. Schneider and a lot of people. That waiter and these fellows."

"Were they ahead of you?"

"Yes, sir. The kitchen's quite a ways down the hall."

"O.K. Give this man your name and address—'n go back to work. Don't move y'r place o' res'dence or change your name or nothin' an' everything'll be all right."

"Yes, sir."

The questioning of the dozen or more men consumed nearly two hours. Reporters left to call their offices with sparse bulletins and returned to listen to the dull routine of stupid denials of unimportant accusations, broken occasionally with a witty or sarcastic sally of the detective. Finally the room was cleared.

"Go down and look over the customers, Joe. Take in anybody with a record."

"*Any*body?"

"Well, use your head *some;* but 'most anybody."

Then with a heavy guard outside the closed door, McQuirk and the doctor tried to reconstruct the crime.

CHAPTER THIRTEEN

M el changed from his cab to a subway, rode to the gang's headquarters and took the newest car, cut through the Holland Tunnel and finally backed between two limousines in a Jersey City storage garage. Then he went to a hotel, left an early call and carefully bolted himself within his room.

How much could McQuirk learn—and how quickly could he learn it? How had he and all that army of police got there so soon? If there hadn't been quite so much trouble he would have preferred to give himself up, to help the police catch Shields. In his mind there was no doubt. Shields had shot the Boss. But as matters stood it was all too dangerous. With the public and the papers and all the comic weeklies screaming for arrests and convictions, somebody might take it into his head to railroad him for political reasons. He wouldn't stand a chance if they wanted to frame him. He was known from coast to coast. He had a nasty record. They held it against him that he had once been a ranger—and later went wrong. *They* didn't know that story. There were no mitigating circumstances for a man like him. He was known to be bad, known to be a killer. No matter what he said nor how many witnesses he had to his innocence, if they wanted to, they could burn him.

And there was Zim. If he gave in Shields' gun and the story of the whole party he would have to tell that Zim was there. Zim's hands were too fresh with the blood of several coppers. They'd prove complicity in that deal, or maybe hang the whole escapade on *him.*

And Chilton. That would come out. In the course of any investigation he aided, it would come out that the reason for the whole party had been to help Chilton leave the United States because he was wanted.

Nope! No matter how much he thought of the Boss. No matter how much he would like to see them catch Shields, he dared not be caught himself; dared not put himself in their power.

He looked his room over carefully, scrutinizing the transom, the windows, the closet. He seemed safe from prying eyes. True, there was only the one exit. In case of serious trouble he would have to fight it out or trust to a three-story drop into an awning. Tomorrow he would try to change his room. The chances for pursuit tonight were not abundant.

That one chesty reporter would, of course, tell McQuirk he had been there. But he had left too soon to be followed so far. They would search his rooms, find nothing, set a dick to watching for him. Trains would be watched. He'd call Happy in the morning and see how serious the whole thing was—politically. That was a contact he would have to keep up now. With the Boss gone, he was the senior member of the mob. Heretofore no one but Poling had been allowed access to Happy. Now it was up to him. If the gang was to be held together, if there was to be any semblance of order in this little army of the shadow-world, he would have to be the general. There was a lot of stock ready to be delivered. Lots of money remained uncollected. Lots of orders remained to be filled. If he was to get his share—and a little more, perhaps—he would have to get busy.

He took Shields' automatic from his pocket and extracted the clip. It was half empty.

Why had the man shot through the door? There was something very strange about that. Why dropped his gun? And where would he go to hide out? Following the old joke about imagining yourself a horse in order to find one which had strayed, Shields might be in the next room. Perhaps he was; it was a hunch. Mel pocketed the gun again and sauntered casually down to look at the register. He was the only guest who had arrived since three in the afternoon.

Bolted once more in his room, he studied the peculiar circumstances that had led to that fusillade of shots that left Poling dead with his gun unfired in his hand. The game little guy! He had drawn *after* he was shot. He had pulled his gun and turned to face an enemy he could not see, *after* he had been killed from behind. It seemed a glorious deed to Mel, something superhuman. A dead man, practically, had started to defend himself. It was a thing he would like to have said of him—when his time came.

He wondered if Chilton had got aboard the ship before the town became so full of police. Had the boat got away? Had Shields rushed there and boarded his own outward-bound vessel? Had Al caught it?

If he wrote the whole story in a letter to McQuirk and mailed it with Shields' gun, could they trace it and catch him?

His head burned and whirled in a mad maze of doubts and half-finished questions. He wished mightily for a drink, remembered a bottle in the door pocket of the car and cursed himself for a fool for leaving it. Suppose it were found! He slept poorly, starting suddenly awake and reaching for his gat a half dozen times before dawn.

CHAPTER FOURTEEN

A policeman and McQuirk's assistant, Carl Denby, supported the nude body of Poling in a position as nearly upright as possible, its back to the door. McQuirk and the doctor squinted at the bloody flesh with their heads near the splintered panel across the room.

McQuirk straightened. "All right. You can let them take him, Doc. I guess there ain't much doubt about what happened. Somebody got a line on him through the key-hole and gave it to him without opening the door. It wasn't anybody in the room. It was somebody with a grudge. Somebody who knew he was here."

"None o' the seven?" Carl asked.

"Not unless one of 'em left the room."

"This ain't the last o' this, by far. If the guys with him were friends, there'll be more killin' b'fore dawn."

The doctor admitted two morgue attendants who covered Poling's body on their stretcher and carried it bumpily down the short flight of steps.

"Try not to scratch them bullets when you take 'em out, Doc. I'll want 'em."

"O.K. I'll try not. Sometimes you can't help it."

"Just do the best you can. I'd like to beat Poling's pals to this next kill, just to show 'em up."

Denby shook his round head in fatalistic dismissal. "You're a right guy, Mac, an' a swell dick, but you ain't got nothin' to work on here. It's a gang killin'. They're all against you—you won't get no help from the office—this Dutchman is scared to talk. There ain't nothin' to do about it."

McQuirk grinned good naturedly. "You think we just ought to forget it, huh? Go home an' go to bed?"

"Might as well. Let these babies kill each other off. The sooner they're gone, the better."

"Listen, Carl, you got wrong. Any time a king gets killed in a racket, somebody else takes his place and all the others just move up one step in line, like buyin' tickets at the Palace. And for every one that goes out *this* way, there's seven more new ones waitin' in the pool halls and speaks to start at the bottom of the easy money ladder.

"It'd be swell if we could start 'em all fightin' each other until they'd all killed each other off, like Jason done—remember, in school?—but it can't be done. The supply's greater'n the demand. Meanwhile—maybe the guy that did this is bumpin' off cops or Chink laundrymen. Nope; the taxpayer's gotta be served.... Anyway, this guy's a respectable plumber—on the surface."

"Aw right, aw right. Let's see y' do it."

"Now, don't dare me, Carl. Get busy. This is your case too."

"Peanuts is my case. I don't even care who done it."

"Listen, boy. Get your body against this job. Get out the mugs of everybody that might of been here tonight."

"The seven?"

"The seven*teen*. All o' the Boss's friends, all o' Shields's gang. Show 'em to the Heinie an' his tough waiter. Don't let 'em sleep. I'll be there later."

"O.K." Carl shoved off, without enthusiasm.

"Keep everybody out. I'm goin' into the silence." McQuirk grinned at the uniformed officer. "Wait outside—shut the door."

Alone in the room, the veteran looked around. It was a game to him—a *big* game. And that night, when he had asked for orders, headquarters had said something that made it still bigger. Instead of the usual "office" to take his duty not too seriously—the kind of instructions he had grown used to receiving in the last two years—there had been a bite in the voice. It had said: "Mac! All bets are off. If Boss Poling's been killed we *want* the guy that did it. Get it? We *want* him."

"I'll get him—if you put it that way."

"Atta boy. It's orders—real orders, see. All bets are off."

"I got you."

Now it was up to him. There would be no legal dodges. If he could get the man or men and the evidence, there would be a conviction. Oh, it was a better game that way. No unfair rules. No favoritism. Man against man. Wit against wit. True, he had the short end of the stick. The others had all the edge. But a handicap made it still more interesting—as long as he could look forward to a conviction. It wasn't much fun to build a network of incriminating facts about a man you knew right along would go free, no matter how guilty he was. McQuirk wondered what had happened at the top of the crooked ladder that led to the new "get your man" order. Well, it was none of his business.

He lit a cigarette and threw the match away. Let's see…

Seven men drinking. Two beer steins. Three whisky glasses. Three…

McQuirk whistled softly to himself as he smelled the contents of three thin glasses. Seltzer—nothing more. Only five drinks. Two men out of the seven did not drink? Two men out of the seven did not enter the room? He continued to whistle softly as he looked at the dirty floor. He'd have the chemist work on those three glasses. Each of them was a third or half full of what smelled like charged water. Two empty cigarette packages disclosed that one man was a Southerner. No one born in New York had ever heard of that brand. McQuirk added those crumpled bits of paper to his little pile of exhibits on the table.

"There ain't a hell of a lot to go on," he muttered. Striking a match, he entered one of the other rooms, found the switch and turned on the light. Dust was thick on the floor. Only in a small semi-circle near the door had it been trampled. Better not walk there much. Have them photographed for prints. Hello!

On the floor at his feet were several playing cards. He picked them up and counted them. Ten. There had been *ten* in the hall. There were *two* on the table. Hastily he compared their backs—all from the same deck, apparently unmarked. "Oh, hell," he sighed. "Another gamblin' row." Then a connection suggested itself. Cards—and gambling—and Chilton, the murderer of one officer and the millionaire Brown. "Oh, oh! An' *he* was a Poling man.

> *"Little Annie Rooney,*
> *Is my sweet-heart."*

He looked into the second room. As dirty as the first, a spot scuffed and trampled near the door—and, glory be, *half* of a card on the floor.

"Ten an' ten is twenty—an' two is twenty-two—an' a half is twenty-two an' a half.

> *"She's my Annie*
> *I'm her Joe*

"Seven men an' five drinks an' twenty-two an' a half cards. Cripes, y' gotta be a math'metician these days." But why scattered around like that? Why in groups of ten?

Let's see. Cops at the door. No windows or doors. Through the café? Get *that* out of Snider. Upstairs? McQuirk opened the door. "Where was them cards y' found, officer?"

"Why, they were over here," pointing, "scattered some. One or two on the step below."

"Um hum. Thanks. Keep the door shut." He ascended the stairs to the floor above and knocked on the door. There was no answer. He heard a soft movement within, drew his revolver and tried the knob. The door was locked.... He backed slowly down the stairs, eyes glued to the knob, his gun trained on the door at the point where a man's heart might logically be—if a man were there.

"What's up?" asked the cop.

"Were any o' you boys up there? Before I got here? Has anybody ..."

"I don't know. I wasn't."

"Get me two men—I'm goin' in." McQuirk's imagination pictured five gunmen waiting silently behind that door.

With two patrolmen, guns in hand, he advanced again to the door of the Schneider apartment. "Listen, in there," he said, raising his voice, "we're coming in. We're police officers an'—an' we're comin' in!"

A key turned—three guns raised. Mrs. Schneider's tear-stained face confronted them. "You take mine man. Vere you take him? He does nothing. I do nothing."

McQuirk touched the brim of his big, soft, black hat. "We'll have to look aroun', Mrs. Snider, an' ask you a few questions."

"Schneider," said the frau testily. "Schneider."

McQuirk took a step forward.

"Easy, chief," cautioned a patrolman. "It may be a blind."

"Have the police been up here before, Mrs. Snider?"

"No."

"Earlier—say an hour ago?"

"No."

"Will you please step aside—while I look around?" He kicked the door wide and stepped into the brilliantly lighted apartment. Every chandelier and fixture was burning.

"You got plenty o' light."

"I was afraid—ven you took mine man avay."

"C'mon, boys." The three searched the apartment.

"Sit down, lady. Were you here all evening?"

"Yes."

"Hear any shooting?"

"Yes."

"What did you do?"

"I ran to the vindow."

"Yeah? See anything?"

"Many police—goming bote vays."

"Anybody come up here?"

"No."

"You sure?"

"You t'ink I'm liar?"

For answer McQuirk walked into the kitchen and returned with ten playing cards in his hand. "Where did these come from?"

"I was playing—some solitary."

"With ten cards?"

"Telling vortunes."

"Where's the rest of 'em?"

"Rest?"

"Where's the rest o' this deck o' cards?"

"I don' know. Those I use."

McQuirk looked at the ten faces. "My wife used to tell fortunes sometimes, Mrs. Snider. I don't remember her usin' the deuce o' diamonds, the ten o' hearts, the ace o' clubs an' jus' these few without no others…. C'mon, quick now! Who's been here? Where'd they go?"

"Nobody iss here."

"Where'd they go? Over the roof? How many?"

"I don' know."

The rapid fire questions rattled her.

"Five men came in here …"

"Four."

"Thanks. An' you let 'em out that trap door in the kitchen…. Up you go, boys. I'll stop the street side."

But their activities were fruitless. The men, of course, had been gone a long time. Mrs. Schneider was taken to the station for further questioning.

"Twenty-two an' a half—an' ten is thirty-two an' a half. That leaves twenty an' a half cards in any good poker deck…. I'll bet seven and a half cents when I find that last half card I'll have my man."

CHAPTER FIFTEEN

The saturnine dope runner known as Al cautiously approached the dock. The night was black. Only the pale yellow glow from a single dim incandescent lamp a block away relieved the inky depths of the squalid, deserted street. A stealthy step ahead of him turned the criminal to stone. He hugged the wall and waited. The soft walking continued, growing louder, then stopped altogether.

A tall figure lounged casually into the lighted area of the inadequate street lamp and stood looking about. The steps proceeded and a man crossed Al's vision only five feet ahead, coming from around the corner of the building which now shielded him.

That was close. A uniformed roundsman joined the two detectives under the lamp and the three moved away together into the blackness, talking in low tones. What the devil were they saying? If he could only have heard! Had the ship left? Could he get close enough to see? How many more bulls were around? If those three men were alone he was all right. He crossed the street, crouching low and running lightly on the balls of his feet. That much was that much. Now—down two short blocks and over one. From the side of the second ware-house he would be able to see the funnels if the ship had waited for him. If it was gone...

But there wasn't much use in coming here. Police were watching every inch of the side of that boat, even if it were there. They'd catch him if he tried to go aboard. But he'd come this far—might as well see it through. Have a hell of a time getting out of this district again if the ship had left. Slowly, tortuously, stealthily, Al maneuvered the three miry blocks across the water-front toward the berth of the vessel which should carry him to Havana for a supply of the precious joy dust. Moving shadows startled him. Twice he had his rod in his hand ready to shoot it out rather than go back to headquarters, but each time the shadow proved harmless and he proceeded deeper and deeper into a district that would have dismayed an honest man in the full light of day. He reached the vantage point from which he could determine if the ship had left him in New York—a hunted, haunted man.

Al was not brave; not very clever. He hit the snow, careful that Old Man Shields did not catch him. As he reached the corner of the brick building he removed his hat and dropped to his knees, peering around the brick wall about two feet from the ground, then he raised up slowly.

The boat was gone.

Between him and the lighter gray of the sky a man's head wearing a uniform cap was silhouetted. What a target! Al got his gun again and took a careful aim. Then—entirely unaware of their mission of mercy—two detectives saved their brother officer's life. They had been watching for the man who would attempt to board that Cuba-bound ship. They had been passing and re-passing in those stinking alleys for an hour or more. It was pure coincidence that they happened, at that crucial moment, to pass that way.

"I'm gonna coffee up," said one—not more than twenty feet from Al's elbow.

"Yeah, this is a bum steer.... He's *on* that boat."

"If they wanted to stop him, honest-to-God, they'd 'a' sent a launch out to board 'er."

At the first syllable, Al dropped his hat over the nickeled barrel of his revolver. To his distraught nerves, that weapon had taken on candle-like properties and was leading these hunters to him. In reality it had reflected what little light there was.

The two voices blurred and mixed with the night sounds of the Bowery, carried on a shore breeze from the west. So they were actually looking for him. But the ship had been allowed to sail, unmolested. He felt the need of a bracer. He was working in the dark in more ways than one. Being in on a racket in an under-dog capacity wasn't so good. He'd be better off jobbing what little snow he could locate right in town. Shields never told anybody anything. Nobody but Slim. *He* was in the know, lucky dog.

Well, now what? Get a phone. Call the Old Man. Ask for orders? Declare himself out of it? Go it alone? The Old Man *could* get him out of a jam. He'd get him out of this one. Slowly and carefully he made his way back to a lighted street. He put twenty blocks between himself and the Bowery before he stopped to phone. He called Shields on the more private wire.

The bell rang a long time. He was about to give it up when a voice answered faintly.

"Hello, Slim?" Al knew it was not Shields.

"Yes."

"Al."

"Yes."

"Seen the Old Man? Is he there?"

"Not yet, why don't you come on up?"

"What for?" Al was a little suspicious.

"I want t' see you."

"What's the address?" A harmless question if he were talking to Slim, a misleading one if the police were in the apartment, answering the phones. He held his breath, waiting for the answer. If a street and number came back over the wire—it was cops, in ambush. But, if it was the police, they were too smart for him. The voice that might easily be Slim's said: "Never mind the hokum. If you're Al you got this address. An' if you're not you won't never get it from me."

"Wait a minute, Slim. Don't get sore. You can see how it is with me. Your voice sounds kinda funny an' I don't want to walk into no hornet's nest."

"Well, they ain't no hornets up here. C'mon up."

Al found a cruising owl cab and gave the address of Shields' apartment.

CHAPTER SIXTEEN

The police department, apparently, was serious about catching the murderer of Clyde Poling. Besides eight men around the water-front, two had been despatched to Shields' place, two to Poling's plumbing shop, two to the home of Bert Melcher, four to the known headquarters of Poling's mob—all before dawn.

On his way to the station McQuirk had studied one of the letters taken from Poling's pocket. Before he started to work on the witnesses he had assembled, he gave the name of its writer to still another team of assistants.

"Dolly—see? At the Solander Hotel on 47th. Bring 'er in." Then he started going over the photographs Carl had taken from the gallery. From fifty he selected twenty. "Let's boil these down so's Snider will come through. If we can knock his pins from under him with the right pictures, we'll get the story fast. If he sees we're guessing, it'll take a month. Them Germans 're hard headed."

"Well, y' can start with Melcher. Y' know *he* was there."

"But he didn't kill his boss. Melcher's a white guy an' Poling's right hand."

"But he was *there*."

"O.K., O.K., yes—he was there. Who else? Zim?"

"Sure. That Polack never misses a shootin'. You can bet he was there."

"Ain't we got a mug of Old Man Shields? That boat business makes me think *he* was in on this."

"There ain't none. The last time we needed it we had to send to Philly. He comes from the city o' brotherly love."

McQuirk picked up a telephone. "Miller!" ... The door opened and an attendant from the fingerprint room yawned against the door-jamb.

"That knife, now, Mr. McQuirk. The Professor's gone home, but he says to tell you that it belonged to Slim Darby."

The telephone. "Miller? ... Send to Philly for mugs an' prints an' records of Shields—Jake Shields—or whatever.... Right away." He hung up the receiver. "Slim Darby? The knife in the Chink's?"

The attendant nodded.

"O.K." Turning to Carl, "You got Slim there?"

"Yeah."

"Put him in. That's another hunch.... An' Chilton ... y' got him?"

"Nope ... He never done nothin' until he crowned this Brown with the bottle. He's only a kid."

"Who'd be likely t' have his pitcher? ... Some dame."

"He run aroun' with a chorus moll—name Patsy."

"Can y' get 'er?"

"I guess so."

"Go get 'er."

"Bring 'er in?"

"Rather steal his pitcher.... See if you can—an' have her watched."

"An' if I can't ..."

"Bring 'er in."

Carl went out with heavy eyes and listless legs. Simon Legree McQuirk, tireless, slave driver, giant. Pounding away all night on a case that would never mean a thing. Well, orders were orders. If he had his way he'd rather go to bed. But McQuirk could go without sleep for a week. Now what was Patsy's last name and where did she live? On 47th, likely; most of those cheap actors did.

McQuirk talked into the 'phone as he turned the photographs over and over on the table. There wasn't much to go on—that was true. No Shields, no Chilton. Only Melcher, Zim, Darby…

"Hello, Phil? … Listen, Phil, do this for me. Go tell this Dutchman Snider that his wife wants to talk to him. Leave the two of 'em alone to chin, see? Get Huck up from the cellar, he knows German. Let him listen in. Don't let on to the old folks that anybody can hear 'em—or understand 'em. The old lady is my best bet an' I think she'll make him talk…. Yeah, now … Right. O.K., Phil…. I'll be down in a few minutes."

Meanwhile, the two men sent to find Dolly stood at the hotel desk.

"That was Miss Cushing who just went out," the clerk told them. The senior member of the team pushed his running mate toward the revolving street door. "Keep 'er in sight." Then turning back to the clerk: "She act funny tonight?"

"She's been calling one number since midnight, but got no answer."

"What number?"

The switch-board attendant copied it for him. The clerk went on: "You'll find her a perfectly decent girl, officer. Of course, I don't know what this trouble is, but Miss Cushing has been here for a long time and I don't think …"

"Thanks." The detective ran with the telephone number in his hand.

Dolly got in a cab. The two men followed in another. "If you don't keep that Yellow in sight we'll send you up for ten years."

The driver grinned. "Shall I run through lights?"

"Swim the river! But don't lose that hack."

Dolly, unable to get Clyde's secret apartment on the 'phone, was going there in person. Her woman's intuition told her something was wrong although the first extras were not yet on the streets and Patsy was out—no one knew where. Unaccustomed to watching her trail, never before followed in her life, unaware of Clyde's major occupation, she paid no attention to the cab which parked thirty feet behind her own. She looked up at the windows. The apartment was dark. Return to the hotel? Wait here? Go up and ring? A heavy dread, without rime or reason, oppressed her heart and shortened her breath. She paid the cab and climbed the ill-lit stairs. It was all on account of George Chilton. It was the police. Clyde had tried to help Patsy's boy friend and got himself in trouble. She heard the hollow buzz of the doorbell in the kitchen as she held the little button down with her thumb. Two men were ascending the stairs. It was late! It was dark! Who were they? Someone who lived in the building. They would pass her by. It was nothing. She pretended to be searching in her bag for a key.

"Hello, Dolly."

They knew her name.

"Hello." Who were they?

"Don't remember me, I guess."

"No—no. I don't."

"Who lives here, Dolly?"

Police! These men were police! Say something! Say *anything*.

"I do."

"Ps-s-st.... Yeah? Alone?"

"What do you mean?"

"Ring the bell again."

"I—I won't."

"No? ... Aw right. *I* will."

There was no answer. "Let's see your keys, Dolly."

They had her. She had no key. No key to an apartment she claimed to be her own. "I—I left 'em inside when I went out…. I've locked myself out."

One man scrutinized the brass circle. "Wrong again, sister; that ain't a spring lock."

"Why—I—"

"Does Poling live here?"

"N-n-no. No—I—I live here, alone."

"What you so scared of, Dolly? We ain't gonna hurt him."

"There ain't nobody gonna hurt him no more," the other man added.

"What do you mean?" She was terror stricken. Something inside was telling her—*this* was the knowledge she had been dreading all evening. This was what she had wanted to know—but had wanted so much *not* to know.

"He's dead."

Everything went black. The words were meaningless. It was as if someone had struck her head with a hammer. She swayed—waiting, waiting, knowing and not knowing. Then she whispered: "Dead."

"Yeah. He was shot—uptown."

"Dead."

"We're tryin't' find the guy that did it."

"Dead."

"You got a key to this?"

"No."

"Shall we bust in?"

The older man shook his head. "No. We'll tell the man on the beat. Then we'll take Dolly in."

She moved between them listlessly to the street. It had happened. It had happened. It had happened. Go with the men. Go anywhere. Nothing mattered now.

On the street she waited with one of the detectives while the other sought the roundsman. Found, he pointed out the apartment. "Hold the fort. Pinch anybody that goes near. So long."

The three drove back to the station.

CHAPTER SEVENTEEN

A city editor finally got a call through to McQuirk.

"Mac! This is Harrison on the *Globe*. I've run out of reporters! Listen, Mac, for heaven's sake tell me where to put 'em to do the most good. I can't keep up with you. You got men all over town. That's no way to do. Where'll I sent one good man to get it all?"

"Ain't you been on that rag long enough to know that one reporter at my desk can do the work o' thirty men on the street? Nothin' ain't gonna happen without *me* knowin' it. Send one o' your bums over here."

"There's four there now."

"Well, call the others in. They're just wastin' their time."

"Thanks, Mac; much obliged."

"Don't mention it."

But McQuirk had reckoned without the heart of a quick-trigger Pole named Zimbronski—or something like that. McQuirk had given all gunmen credit for enough sense to hide in time of trouble. He had not seen a gun *kicked* from Zim's hand. For all his knowledge of killers and their ways, he would have been helpless before the revelation that such an action may breed respect in some twisted minds.

For Zim was not hiding. Zim was not standing on Broadway, pulling traffic officer's sleeves to attract attention to himself, but he was not hiding. And McQuirk had reckoned—in speaking to the city editor—without taking into consideration that wherever in this world Zim happened to be, there was potential news. For Zim had in him the lay equivalent of what is the "nose for news" in a reporter. He had a "hand for creating news"—and at that moment that hand was stroking the head of a big Belgian shepherd dog while his other kept his automatic from slipping off his lap.

He had no business in Shields' apartment. Shields would have been disappointed in his dog for tolerating the fellow's presence. But there he was—and the dog was friendly. Carl Denby had told McQuirk that their quest for a missing killer would have its objective changed before dawn. It was his theory that a friend of Poling would deliver the answer to that mystery into their hands in the form of a corpse. Then they would have an entirely different man to hunt. And that might go on indefinitely. Each new murder would solve the last, but the crooks would always be one jump ahead of the law.

Here was Zim, waiting to substantiate that line of reasoning. He rubbed the rough ears of the huge dog and watched the door. The phone rang—again. A dodge? Would they be at the door at the same time? He backed to the instrument, his gun in readiness. If the knob turned…

"Hello," very softly.

"Al again, Slim."

"Yes."

"I can't get in. There's two dicks acrost the street watchin' the house. You better watch your step."

"I will."

"Say, you ain't Slim."

"No?"

"Well, y' don't sound like it."

"I can't help that. I gotta keep my voice down. They don't know I'm here."

"Well, what'll I do, Slim?"

"Find the Old Man."

"How in hell can I find him?"

"Look around. Go to Bill's."

"I'm *in* Bill's."

Zim thought fast. Al was in Bill's. He had seen neither Slim nor Shields. The police would get around there later, sure. Maybe he could beat them.

"Has Bill seen the Old Man?"

"No."

"You wait there for me."

"Wait here?"

"Sure—an' if the Old Man comes in, tell him I'm on my way."

Al turned from the telephone, walked around the partition that separated the back room from the bar. Slim was just tossing off a drink. Al stood next to him at the busy bar. "Let's get out o' here, Slim. We're bein' framed."

"Yeah?"

"I'll say so. C'mon. Quick."

Slim tossed money down and followed the excited man to the street. "I just had the house on the 'phone. Somebody there claimed to be you. I didn't think it was you, but I wasn't sure."

"Did you say anything?"

"Not a thing. I told him I was in Bill's."

"How the hell did they get in—with the mutt there? He hates a copper. He'd kill a copper."

"Unless the coppers killed him."

Slim's long fingers grasped his companion's bicep. "Do you think they did? Do you think those yellow skunks would hurt that dog?" His knuckles cracked under the pressure of his grip.

"Jesus, leggo my arm."

"D' y' think they did?"

"How would I know? There's somebody there, makin' out he's *you*. 'At's all I know."

"I'm goin' over there, Al. I'm goin' over an' see."

"There's two dicks acrost the street."

"Where?"

"No, no ... I mean by the house."

"Watchin' the door ..."

"I wouldn' try it, Slim. Let's get the hell out o' this. I guess I'll go back to Washington."

"You missed the boat."

"Yeah, the bastards."

"I wonder if that Kid caught it."

"What kid?"

"Chilton, the dealer. Poling's dealer that socked the guy with the bottle."

"Was he makin' for that boat?"

"Sure, that's what started the trouble."

"Y' know—I don't see no sense in this mess. What'd the Old Man want to get Poling for? An' how come he dropped 'is gat? I ain't too sure the Old Man's safe, Slim?"

"Neither am I. I'm goin' to the house. T' hell with the dicks. J got to see that dog."

"Not me.... So long, big boy."

"So long."

As the two men parted, Zim was making news. Five blocks from Billy's saloon he had descended the inside front steps, holding the big dog by the collar. He had no plan but he had heard that this animal hated policemen and could be trusted to handle his share if need arose. At the foot of the steps he stood for five minutes, waiting for an idea. The detectives Al had told him were there were not in sight. That meant nothing. They were watching from a window. The idea was slow in coming. Without exposing himself to view he tried to locate the eyes he knew were focused on that doorway. Nothing happened. The dog became restive. A cab turned the corner and approached the house next door to where he stood. A drunk clambered out and fussed about finding the money. Zim watched, on his toes for a sprint at exactly the right time. The farewaved the chauffeur a tipsy farewell and the gears shifted.

"So long, boy," Zim whispered to the dog. "You'll have to shift for yourself." He patted his gray flank and leaped on the running board of the car. "Don't stop. Go ahead!"

Feet were running on the sidewalk. A roar like a lion's split the quiet night. Zim crawled into the cab as it sped on—and looked out the little window in the rear.

A gray streak was bounding in the opposite direction. One man was helping his companion to his feet. A dog to be proud of! Where would the poor mutt go? He seemed to be going somewhere in a hurry. "Turn the corner." A moment later: "This'll do." When he paid him: "Now get out o' this neighbourhood quick, if you know what's good for you."

He walked rapidly toward Billy's bar. A shield and brass buttons slowed his step. He turned and doubled back toward Broadway. It must be five o'clock—maybe later. He looked at the eastern sky. Dawn was streaking it gray. A fool's errand. Why bother? He was tired, sleepy. Grab a paper and go back to Henry Jackson's room on 6th Avenue. His guts were gone. He needed a drink. The speaks were always full of cops at this hour. The word would be out by now—to bring him in. He took a chance on a camouflaged cigar store. Poling's murder was the topic of conversation. He drank three jolts of Scotch as quickly as possible and left the place feeling better. A cop nodded to him as he left the place. What do you know about that? Scared of nothing. "One of each," he said to the newsy and walked on to his hotel.

CHAPTER EIGHTEEN

"Did he get you? You hurt?"

"Went right for my throat. Jeez, what a dog. He weighs a ton."

"Let's see."

The two detectives moved to a street lamp and looked for wounds. They were slight, but the trick had been turned. Zim had got away.

"Who was that came out?"

"I couldn't see. That damn cab ..."

"Yeah—look! Who's 'at?"

Slim had turned into the dark doorway.

"Let's go."

They loosened their irons as they crossed the street. A key was turning in a lock above them. They waited. The door closed. They creaked up the steps. "Shall we wait?"

"No." The man who had been bitten knocked with his gun on the door.

"If you come in," Slim said, "come in with your hands over your head."

"That you, Darby?"

"Yes.... Where's my dog?"

"Open the door. Somebody jus' came an' let your dog out."

"Who came an' let 'im out?"

"We don' know. He got away."

"I don't believe a damn word of it.... Where's that dog?"

"Let us in, Slim."

"Like hell I will."

"We got orders, Slim. You're wanted at the office."

"I know…. Where's the mutt?"

"Forget the mutt. He chewed a piece out o' my face."

"Yeah? That's music to my ears. He always did hate cops."

"Like you, eh?"

"Yes, like me."

"We got you cornered, Slim. You might as well come along without wakin' the neighbors."

There was a long silence.

"I'll tell you what I'll do, boys. When I hear that pup bark outside this door I'll open the door an' give up without trouble. Until I do hear him you can sit there an' rot."

"We ain't got your dog. He ran away."

"Who let 'im out?"

"A little guy. Honest t' God, Slim. We was across the street an' all of a sudden out they come. The little guy hopped on a cab and the dog come after Harry here. We beat him off an' he ran like blue blazes down the street."

"How long ago?"

"Just now. Not more'n three minutes."

"Somebody's been in here, all right. Oh, nuts, it was you guys. Nope! It don't work so easy. Bring back the dog—or come an' get me. Take your choice."

"You know we can get you."

"Yeah, I know. But what about me gettin' you while you're at it? You yellow skunks! You'd send for the army. The two of you'd never try to take me. Not two guys that'd pick on a dog."

There was no answer to that. No answer of words. The gage had been thrown down. If they were men they must take it up.

His companion pushed Harry aside, took careful aim at the voice where they had heard it last—and pulled.

The report died away.

"Try it again, you louse. You missed me."

Both detectives fired through the door. Slim ran to the front window. The street was still deserted. What should he do? If they caught him now—these two, without witnesses—he'd get the works. Better shoot it out. He was their match. His left hand needed target practice. He drew both of his guns and slid along the wall to the door. Both men were working on the lock. It sprung and the door swung back, opening in. Slim let Harry have it first. He dropped. The other man ran to the stairs for some protection.

"Come on, you heels! Come on, dog killers. You want any more?" A bullet glanced from a door hinge and tore away half of his ear. He went blind with rage. All thought of caution left him and he stormed into the open hallway after the man who was as yet unhit. It did not occur to him that Harry was still danger-ous. He poured lead with both hands at the second man who fled half-way down the stairs, then pitched and fell, screaming at the bottom. But Harry was not out. Painfully he lugged his revolver from beneath his crumpled body and with the last cartridge in it, sent Slim sliding headlong after the man he had killed.

CHAPTER NINETEEN

The papers Zim bought had very little news for him. They were largely bulletins and scare heads. Of the few "facts" they gave, half—at least—were false. But a few hours later, the first editions of the afternoon sheets were blazing with it. Crime and the law had entered the death grapple. It was being settled once and for all—amid leaden pellets and showers of blood—which should rule the city, the clean or the unclean.

The Globe:

GALLANT POLICE STAND
BREAKS CRIME WAVE

"BOSS" POLING DEAD
FIVE ARE HELD

John (Slim) Darby and Detective Brenner in Hospital

STAGE DEAD

The cohorts of organized crime are in hiding or mourning today following a series of raids engineered by Deputy Commissioner Martin, spurred on by the murder of Clyde (Boss) Poling and the death of Thomas L. Brown of Flint, Michigan. Commissioner Martin could not be found by the thousands of friends who wished to congratulate him today. His statement to the press, made at one o'clock this morning, following the Poling murder, rang the knell for all gangsters and gunmen in this city.

"I am going to clean up this town and send these so-called bad men back where they came from if I have to hire a brand new police force. Graft is at an end. There are enough loyal men in the uniform of our great peace-time army to keep this city clean. I mean to see that they have an opportunity to do so."

There followed a long red, white and blue account of the commissioner's good deeds and his plans for the future.

In another column:

TWO-GUN MAN FROM
TEXAS FIGHTS IT OUT
WITH POLICE

John (Slim) Darby, a well-known desperado who arrived here from Texas several years ago, is dying in the Swedish-American Hospital from bullet wounds he received in a finish fight with Detectives Patrick Stage and Harry Brenner. Wanted for complicity in the murder of Lee Sin, a Chinese laundry proprietor killed night before last and as a material witness in the murder of the notorious "Boss" Poling last night, the doughty "Slim" was trailed to his home and cornered by the two officers.

Neither Darby nor Brenner could make comprehensive statements due to their critical conditions. But the blood-stained hallway and bullet-splintered doors at 306 Barth Plave gave mute testimony to the bitterness of the struggle.

EYE-WITNESS TELLS STORY

John Kooster, a machinist living in the building, was roused from sleep at five-thirty this morning by the sound of gun fire in the second floor hall of the building. The shooting, he says, was centered about the door of the apartment occupied by Mr. Darby and an older man whose name he did not know. Mr. Kooster remarked that until last night a big police dog had been the constant companion of these two men. It was unaccountably missing at the time of the shooting.

It was said at police headquarters that the older man who had occupied the apartment with Darby was Jake Shields, dope king and leader of a gang. He also is missing.

Mr. Kooster's story follows:

"They seemed to be shooting through the door at first. Stopping to talk and swear between shots. Then they got the door open and Mr. Darby came out, shooting with both hands. Mr. Brenner dropped. I thought he was dead, but he wasn't. Then Mr. Darby drove the other man down the steps and apparently killed him. When he fell he yelled bloody murder. Then Mr. Brenner got on one knee and shot Mr. Darby from behind.

"That was all. The three of them just lay there groaning. I called the police and we tried to make Mr. Brenner drink some water, but he couldn't. They stayed unconscious until the ambulance came."

A police stenographer and a detective are at the bedside of Darby, waiting for a last-minute rally when a death-bed confession can be expected.

On the other side of the page:

POLING MURDER
NOT GAMBLING QUARREL

Lieutenant McQuirk
Promises Arrest of Guilty
Party in Twenty-four Hours

Lieutenant of Detectives Jerome P. McQuirk, in charge of the investigation of the murder of Clyde (Boss) Poling in a Yorkville cabaret shortly after midnight last evening, sent his witnesses home at noon today. He had, he said, learned all that they could tell him. "There is no need of holding these people here," he said. "They all have homes and business duties. They have given me all the information they have. We are almost certain to have the guilty parties in cells within twenty-four hours."

Pressed for details of his suspicions and the findings of the investigation carried on behind closed doors all through the night and well into the morning, the veteran of the bureau said: "There was no gambling done in the room that night. The meeting was a conference of gang leaders, probably called to muster their forces against the police in the concerted effort now being made to drive this element from the city. What the results of their conference was, it is difficult to say. We are almost certain that Slim Darby, now in the Swedish-American

Hospital, was among those present. If the doctors can revive him sufficiently to obtain a statement, it may shorten our search for the murderer."

POLING'S SWEETHEART WEEPS

Miss Dolly Cushing, the beautiful young actress, sweetheart of Clyde Poling, the plumbing contractor, sobbed out her story of misplaced affection, at police headquarters.

"I didn't know he was bad," she kept repeating as tears dimmed her child-like eyes. "He was always very good to me. I met him at a party. I thought he was a plumber—or maybe a bootlegger. I can't believe he was a gang leader like you say."

The girl is said to have revealed a secret apartment of Poling's as well as other facts which the police withheld for purposes best known to them.

It is alleged that the search is now confined to two individuals, one Jake Shields, known to his cronies as "Old Man" Shields, the room-mate and pal of John Darby, and one Mike Zimbronski, a Polish retainer of Boss Poling's and one time bodyguard of the notorious Packy McDowell.

Shields and Poling have long been rivals for the underworld crown. That struggle for supremacy in gangland is advanced as sufficient motive for Shields to have done the deed. Zimbronski, it is alleged, arrived at the conference very drunk and was heard muttering threats as he entered the room.

Bert Melcher, once of the Texas Rangers and now Poling's right-hand man, is also missing. His photograph has been positively identified by three witnesses as one of the men in attendance at the scene of the crime.

MRS. SCHNEIDER CONFESSES

It was revealed by Mrs. Hilda Schneider, wife of the cabaret owner, that four men effected their escape through a trap door in her apartment, thence across the roof-tops. She has identified three of these men as Melcher, Darby and Zimbronski. She was doubtful of the fourth. She will be asked to view a photograph of Jake Shields when it arrives from Philadelphia where that worthy has a police record.

It is said to be one of the marvels of the local underworld that Shields has attained his present position of power as a racketeer without leaving a trace of evidence to warrant his arrest by local authorities. He has served several terms in the penal institutions of other states, notably Pennsylvania. He has been mentioned in connection with the shooting of Lee Sin, Chinese, night before last. Positive identification of Darby as a party to that killing was expected this afternoon when Sam Kee, a young Chinese student, will view the wounded man at the hospital.

No arrests have been made in connection with the wholesale butchery of police and federal operatives in the Bronx night before last, although it is known that the arrest sought by the police ambush that night was none other than Clyde Poling. A round-up of his retainers and henchmen is in progress and witnesses of that crime will view the suspects tomorrow.

POLING'S PASSING NOT MOURNFUL

The taking of Boss Poling by a member of the world he served was a fitting death for so great a criminal. The state has sought his apprehension for three months or more to answer questions upon several counts. He has enjoyed liberty for eight years, always proving alibis or squeezing through the meshes of the legal net upon some technicality or other upon the few occasions that he has been brought to trial.

In addition to his indirect responsibility for the slaughter of the men in the Bronx, Poling is alleged to have owned the gambling house in which Thomas L. Brown and Detective Gilray were killed by George Chilton two weeks ago. Chilton is still at large.

Poling's hand was seen in two-thirds of the criminal activities of this city. His death is a distinct advantage to the forces of law and order.

But there was one newspaper whose politics did not agree with the City Hall administration and it seized this opportunity to hold the authorities up to ridicule and scorn.

What, one editorial writer wanted to know, was half the police force doing wandering around the docks all night while their fellows were shot to bits by a two-gun man from the west? Why were they concentrated there, when everyone knew that the ship they might be watching had been allowed to sail from port with the blessings of the police—within a very short hour after Poling's death? That paper wanted to know a lot of things that no one dared tell.

McQuirk read their diatribe and shook his sandy head. It was all true. All their recriminations, all their charges, all their aspersions. But he could do nothing but follow the course he was on, as best he could. He called the office of that paper on the phone and asked for the reporter on the Poling case. "Come over here, Guy. Want to talk to you."

Guy Field of the *Register* came running. "Hello, Mr. McQuirk; something hot?"

"Yeah—sit down, sonny."

"Thanks."

"Have a smoke."

"Thanks."

"I—I liked your story in the afternoon paper.... Liked it a lot."

"I'm glad you did, thanks.... I wasn't sure how you'd take it."

"I take it all right.... I like your attitude; like your independence. Liked that editorial too."

"Gee, that's fine."

"I could bust you for it, if I wanted to, you know.... If I didn't like it."

"Well—"

"Well, hell! You know I could."

"Well—"

"But I don't want to. I feel like you're doing something worth while, raisin' so much stink about graft and the fellows in the soft berths. I'd like to fight 'em too. I feel like you fellows on the *Register* are helping me, personally.... This is all confidential, of course. And so I'm going to do you a favor. Kind of a return favor."

The telephone rang at McQuirk's elbow.

"I'll tell you what I'm goin' to do." He ignored the ringing bell.

Guy motioned toward the instrument but the big man waved it aside. "Let it ring. I want to give you this for your next edition, see. The man that killed Clyde Poling ain't no *man* at all…. It's a woman!"

Then, leaving the reporter to get over the shock of his announcement he reached for the phone, winking one enormous eye broadly and screwing up one corner of his big mouth.

"Hello!" he shouted into the phone.

PART THREE

CHAPTER TWENTY

Young Field watched the smiling visage of the weathered detective slowly lose its joviality, sag a moment, and harden into lines and furrows of disgust, hatred and scorn. After saying—yelling—"Hello," he did not speak for more than a minute—two minutes. Then he sighed heavily. A voice at the other end of the telephone wire finally stopped. "Yes, sir," he said at last. "I understand perfectly." Then he hung up and squinted at the reporter. "I just gave you some *news*, boy. Big news. Why don't you get out of here with it? Come on, beat it. Run! But don't forget, all that stuff about agreein' with your editorial is just between *us*. Don't let *that* get out."

"But is that all? Aren't you going to tell me who she is?"

McQuirk looked at the telephone, then back at Guy. "Not on your life. And the sooner you get out of here, the better for both of us…. Scoot!"

It was ten minutes after the reporter had left before the telephone rang again. McQuirk had not moved from his chair. The voice of his superior still sounded in his ears, saying all of the things he had dreaded to hear. Calling him off, just when he was getting somewhere. Knocking him down just as he was about to open a door that had been sealed to him for years. Here was the long arm of graft again, the gold-tipped fingers of corruption. It must be Shields. It must have been Shields' gold that seeped into the high and mighty circle to close the case. Maybe he was wrong about that girl. Maybe she hadn't done the actual shooting. Or—if she had—maybe she was Shields' sweetheart. However it was, she held the secret. If he could have found her before he got that order they wouldn't have dared call him off. If he could have got her story and given it to the papers—no man in the city could have stopped the wheels of the law, no matter how high he was nor how much money he was paid. But she had disappeared. Perhaps sailed—with official sanction—on that Cuba-bound ship. He could have learned that, given time. Now it was all off. What had he said? "The lid is on again, Mac." The lid. Damn that lid! It was that lid that made all these killings possible. It was that lid which kept him down like a stewing potato at the bottom of the pot. If he could only reconcile himself to begin grabbing with the rest. If only his heart was crooked—he could be sitting on the lid with the others.

"Call in your men. The Poling case is closed. Tell the papers nothing. Tell them we are awaiting developments."

Awaiting developments! Awaiting the Judgment Day! They made him sick. Then the phone rang again.

"Boss—this is Davis. Where the devil is that bird with the Chink? We've had Darby almost conscious twice. They ought to be out here in case he comes to."

"Oh, yeah. Sure. Sit there at the phone, Davis. I'll find out what's keepin' 'em." He called downstairs.

"Have they taken that Chinese kid out to the hospital yet?"

"He ain't goin', Mac. We got orders from the big fellow not to send 'im."

"That—that's right. I was afraid maybe he'd gone a'ready."

There it was again. Hush, hush, hush. Nothing to do. He called the hospital back and got Davis. "Listen, boy, your wife is very sick. You'll have to run home an' see 'er."

"*My* wife! I ain't married, Mac."

"All right, then it's that steno's wife. Tell him his wife has a convulsion an' he's to go on home."

"Oh, I getcha."

"An' your lumbago is suddenly worse. See? Go home an' put on a mustard plaster."

"What about the Chink?"

"He's crooked too. He run away."

"How about gettin' a week off, Mac? I'd like to see a fellah in Albany."

"Not the Governor!"

"No, another fellah."

"Go ahead."

"Thanks, Mac.... What shall I tell the doc?"

"Tell 'im to let Slim die in his own way an' not to torture him no more."

"O.K."

Two receivers were replaced.

And to think he was being a party to this outrage. The very thought sickened his stomach. Good men could be slaughtered thus. Yes, even Slim was a good guy. What a business!

"By God, I'll quit!" He reached for pen, ink and paper. "I'll get out o' this. It ain't a white man's work."

The door opened and Carl Denby grinned at him, his moon face lighted with infectious merriment. "Hyah, Mac. How's it go?"

"You must 'a' heard the news."

"Yeah, I heard; what'd I tell you?"

Mac shook his head. "I never thought they dared."

"I knew. They can do anything. What did they say?"

"'The Poling case is closed.' Wouldn't that get your nanny?"

"Not mine. Y' want my report?"

"Yeah—where is she?"

"She's disappeared. Blown. Gone. There ain't a trace.... I think she got on that boat with Chilton."

"Yeah? Who told you Chilton made the boat?"

"Why, didn't he?"

"Maybe."

"Well, she left the hotel about noon yesterday, just like Dolly said. Nobody knows where she was or what she did until she turns up at Schneider's and leaves with the Kid. Are you sure your tip is straight that she came back the second time?"

"A dishwasher gave me that. Nobody else saw her. He was out in back o' the kitchen smokin' when she ran out with the Kid. She was hardly out of sight when a man come in, rushin' like somebody was after him. He was there only a minute or so when this Patsy came back.

"He went back in the kitchen then, and before he could cross the room he heard the shots. Then, instead of steppin' outside again—where he could see somethin'—he followed the cooks and waiters into the hall—an' she went out the way she came in."

"With Shields?"

"Prob'ly."

"Well, what'll I do? Dolly's bein' shadowed. The theater, plumbin' shop and three apartments are under surveillance. If I was you I'd cable Cuba—that is, if you're goin' any farther with it."

"I'm not.... I can't.... I'm writin' my resignation."

"Hell you are!"

"You think I'm goin' t' let the newspapers laugh me out o' town? If I quit now I'm on top o' the world. In a week I'd be a mangy goat. I'm gettin' out while the gettin' is good."

"But what about me? What'll I do?"

"You'll take my place. It's a step up for you. If you play ball they'll make you keeper o' the lid an' some day you'll be rich."

"Shall I call all the boys in?"

"All of 'em. Take my calls for a while—tell 'em all to report back here in person."

"No more pinches?"

"Not another pinch."

"Dolly?"

"Let 'er hang 'erself."

Then McQuirk began to write.

CHAPTER TWENTY-ONE

Melcher drove his car on to the Dyckman Street ferry and set his brakes. They wouldn't be waiting or watching up there, and it was close to the hospital. He was on his way to see Slim. If they'd let him talk to Slim—and the man was able to talk—he'd give himself up after the confab. He wanted the low-down on the shooting. He wanted Slim's version of Poling's death. He wanted to learn, if possible, where Shields might be hiding. A dying man had few secrets. Then, there was the brotherhood of "the border". They had been on opposite sides of the fence down there, but Slim had been a square crook. And Mel had to admit to himself that Slim's shooting left hand had always called for a certain respect.

He left his car long enough to try for the ninth time since ten o'clock to get Happy on the phone. As before, there was no answer. That was very peculiar. He knew he was calling the right number. He had heard Poling call it a hundred times. No answer. He drove on to the hospital and as he slammed the car-door, looked around the entrance for a familiar face or figure from headquarters. None was visible. "That's funny."

There was no objection to him seeing Mr. Darby, but he must be very quiet. Was he a relative? "Yes," Mel lied, "he's my nephew."

There was no detective at the door of the room. Mel frowned in disbelief. This wasn't according to Hoyle. A gunman was dying! He had information the police wanted—and there were no cops in sight? It was a mystery to Mel.

The room smelled heavily of drugs and the white bed seemed more like a bier in the pale half-light of early evening.

Slim's eyes were closed, his breathing short, fluttery, labored. "Has he come to?"

"Oh, yes. He has been conscious for over an hour."

"Can I talk to him?"

"Not long."

"No …"

Slim's eyes opened and his thin lips twisted in an effigy of a smile.

"Mel," he whispered. " 'Lo, *hombre*."

"Hello, Slim. How y' feel?"

"Spine," he gritted between his teeth. "Lead in my spine…. All up."

"Naw, you'll be all right…. Why ain't nobody with you?"

"Case closed." Slim smiled again, very painfully. "Called off—account—don't dare—m-m-m-m." His speech blurred into a groan.

"Where's Shields, Slim?"

The man in bed shook his head.

"I hate to torture you, old pal, but I gotta know. Did *he* get the Boss?"

"I don' know."

"You wouldn't lie *now*."

"No use."

"How come you t' get it?"

"They took the mutt."

"Yeah? The swine! An' you shot it out—for the mutt?"

"I got two of 'em. Wisht it was twenty."

"Y' make a statement yet?"

Again Slim shook his head. "Ain't goin' to. They don't want none."

"Any idea where your Old Man might be—for my personal reasons?"

"No idea…. Think they got him."

"Think who got 'im?"

"Chinks."

"Yeah?!"

Slim nodded. "Tong or somp'n. Y' know?"

"I never thought o' that."

"I did. Think they got Poling too—accident."

"Say! That's an idea!"

The nurse looked in. "You'll have to go now. He can't talk any more. He's very weak."

There was something terrible in Slim's hand clasp. He held Mel's fingers with a desperate grip—as if he would hold on to something healthy and strong and earthy as long as possible.

"So long, Slim. I'll come see you again tomorrow—if you ain't got the wrong kind o' visitors."

The Texan's twisted grin returned and he shook his head again. "Y' wouldn't kid me, Mel…. I won't be here tomorrow. So long, fellah."

"So long."

Mel stumbled frantically toward the fresh air. Damn that ether! Automatically, he looked both ways before opening the door. No police.

That was a hot one. Somebody had got to Happy and it was all fixed. No use hiding any more. He would drive past the hang-out and see if this was on the level.

Poor Slim. He was done. Finished because the cops took a dog. Not even *his* dog. The mutt belonged to Shields. Some guys were like that.

The door to the Poling headquarters was locked with a padlock, just as he had left it. There were no detectives in sight.

Monahan, on the beat for years, had just finished pulling the box. He recognized the slow-moving car and waved a friendly greeting. Mel stopped.

"Sir to *you*," said the officer.

"And you," Mel rejoined. "What's the good word?"

"The good wurrrd? Ha! The good wurrd'll be 'save y'r money'," and he laughed uproariously.

Mel waited for him to overcome his mirth at his own wit. Serious, at last, he bent close to the car with one foot on the running board. "What d'ye want t' know, me boy?"

"I read in the papers I was wanted."

"Sure, y' can't believe thim paypers! Not *never*."

"C'mon, Pat. What's the dirt?"

"The dirt is that I'm t' keep the peace in these parts an' let no man insult no woman on *my* beat."

"Honest?"

"Honest? I'm always honest."

"Y' mean, they're droppin' the case? They ain't gonna look for the guy that killed the Boss! Is that it?"

"Not so loud, me boy…. Yeah. That's it."

"Well I'll be damned if I drop it!"

"They'll be expectin' that too, I'm afraid."

"Yeah, that's their style. Let us get our own man. All right, by God, I will!"

"Are y' knowin' who it was, then?"

"I've got a damned good idea."

"Shields, mebbe?"

"Maybe. I'll see you later, Pat. I got a date to kill a Chinaman."

"Mebbe *that's* no stage joke!"

"Hm, maybe not…. G'night."

"Olive oil, me boy. See y' in the dock."

So it *was* true. It was a "gang killing"—let the *gang* fight it out. All right! He'd begin with Shields. Where would that bird go? Washington? He tried once more to get Happy and this time he was informed that "the line has been disconnected".

Now what did that mean? Had Happy called the cops off? Or was it someone else? Was it all a ruse to trip the guilty man? What had made Happy draw in his shell? If he, Mel, could not reach the throne room by phone, how could anyone else?

Mel worried his way through traffic, fretful that there could be activity or the cessation of activity without his knowledge. This was no way to do business. He had to know where he stood. He parked his car a block from Detective Headquarters, locked his own gun securely inside and carried Shields' in his hand, wrapped in newspapers. It might have been shoes on their way to a cobbler.

Two plain-clothes men on their way out of the building nodded pleasantly. Mel's contempt for all this obfuscation and chicanery increased. He confronted the man on duty at the desk. "Is McQuirk in?"

"Hello, Bert."

Hello, Bert! As if he were a brother-in-law or a cousin, dropped in to pass the time of day. "Is McQuirk here?"

"Nope. He just went out. Anything I can do for you?"

Melcher stood staring at the man so long, his mouth twisted in a mirthless, sarcastic smile, that the situation became funny to both of them. "Oh, Lord," the detective laughed. "Go 'way, you're killing me!"

"Well, say, now; this may be a scream to you, but I want to see Mac."

"He ain't here."

"Where can I reach 'im?"

"At his home."

"Give me the number."

"No monkey shines, Bert. Mac ain't lookin' for trouble. You'll find him—the same as always towards you."

"I know. I won't do anything to upset him. I'm no child."

The man wrote an address and telephone number on a slip of paper. "So long, Bert."

"So long."

"By the way, Bert. Do you know who it was?"

"On the level?"

"On the level."

"I wish t' God I did."

"'At's what we thought."

The door closed behind him.

CHAPTER TWENTY-TWO

The *Register* scooped the other evening papers with its exclusive statement from McQuirk that a woman had killed Boss Poling. But it was the "bull-dog" edition of the *Gazette* that beat the other morning papers to his resignation.

All of the morning papers carried the story of Slim Darby's death at 9:30 P.M. He had made no statement. But the *feature* story was about the girl; about Patsy, who could not be found.

Patsy Shelling, soubrette in several past Broadway hits, rehearsing—until the day of Poling's murder—in a big, new, musical comedy, had disappeared, carrying with her the great secret of the underworld. Not only the police, but all of crookdom wanted that secret. Although McQuirk had not named her, it was thought he suspected her of the actual perpetration of the crime. By devious means it had been learned that not one of Poling's friends or his enemies could say certainly who had fired the fatal shots.

Dolly Cushing, Patsy Shelling's room-mate and sweetheart of Poling, was prostrated under the double grief of her lover's death and her friend's disappearance. It was insinuated that Patsy also loved Clyde Poling and that she had killed him through jealousy. Patsy's connection with George (Kid) Chilton had not yet been brought to light.

Then, from day to day, the space devoted to these matters became less and less as the inactivity of the police fed no new fuel to the blaze. McQuirk refused to be interviewed; Bert Melcher appeared again in Broadway night clubs; Deputy Commissioner Martin was out of the city on a fishing trip with friends. Dolly went back to her place in the chorus line; Jake Shields, Mike Zimbronski and George Chilton remained among the missing. No one paid any attention to Al Turner. He was never seen, but if he had been the papers would have ignored it. Slim Darby was saved from an ignominious burial by the generosity of an anonymous friend who deposited five hundred dollars with an undertaker with complete instructions for interment in San Antonio, Texas.

There the news stopped. In his cups, Bert Melcher would defy Jake Shields to show his face; but the novelty of that bravado wore off after a few repetitions and the Poling case drifted into a journalistic limbo. Eight days after the murder scarcely a reference could be found in any of the city dailies.

But the publisher of the *Register* who wrote his own editorials and had political aspirations was not content.

The Federal Government, in the person of the Prohibition Enforcement Officer of the moment, was not content.

The publisher called Guy Field into his highly-polished office. "Young man," he said, "I want you to get in to his home to see McQuirk. I want to hire him…. Just a minute. I want to hire him privately to get at the bottom of this Poling case. I'm going after the City Hall if it takes every penny I own, but this time I'm going to do it right. No editorials. No news. We'll work under cover—with McQuirk—until we have the story complete from start to finish. Then we'll spring it and watch the smoke.

"He's a fighter, Field. He's a smart detective. I think he'd have solved this mystery if he'd been given a chance. What's more, I think he *wants* to. My money will let him…. Go see. Go and ask him. I'll pay anything he asks. He mustn't be seen coming here, however. That would tip them off.... And the other papers mustn't get it."

"It's a peach of an assignment, Mr. Scott. I see only one difficulty."

"What's that?"

"Well, everybody knows McQuirk. No matter how much he tried to keep under cover, everybody would know he was up to something if he went nosing around. I suggest that you let him be the brains—but that you authorize him to get help—any help he needs for outside work."

"Oh, certainly, certainly. That's understood."

On the same afternoon, the spokesman for the committee of inquiry appointed by the Federal branch of law enforcement to scrutinize the police activities in connection with Zim's highly theatrical evening in the Bronx laid down the law to McQuirk's successor, the tractable Mr. Carl Denby.

"We've gone as far as we can in a friendly fashion. We have written your department our last letter. Unless you do something about this within a week it will go out of our hands and the Supreme Court or the Senate or somebody will take action against the city government."

"But what can I do? The man escaped. We don't know who he was. Who shall I arrest?" Carl was playing for time.

"You have his hat. You have his shoes. You have a good description of him and three or four witnesses who could identify him.

"You can be just as slow to catch Poling's murderer as you care to. That's none of our business. But unless you get busy on this other case, Washington will have something to say that will singe your whiskers."

"Well," said the detective, "I don't know why you're telling me all of this. I'm not running the police department."

"I'm trying to save you big trouble. We can settle it ourselves or we can let it go on up to the big fellows and become a national issue. Get next to yourself. Let's put somebody away for that job and save a devil of a lot of trouble."

"I guess you're right." Carl picked up his telephone. "Hello, Chuck…. Say, go get Zimbronski. I want to talk to him."

CHAPTER TWENTY-THREE

B ert Melcher sat at his regular corner table in the French Frolic night club, his back to the wall, his eyes moving slowly but ceaselessly from one end of the room to the other. The dance floor was crowded with jouncing couples, all intent upon the great task of making time fly. Mel sipped a drink and watched, just waiting. A color wheel revolved on a spotlight, throwing the faces of the dancers into pools of red, blue, orange, green and purple. Almost everyone was in evening dress, including the grizzled Melcher and the young man who also sat alone at the next table. This stranger laughed and shook his head, as if he enjoyed a comic scene no one else could see. He looked at Mel.

"When that green light hits 'em they look so damned sick," he said as if apologizing for his mirth.

Mel grinned and looked back at the dance floor. It was true. He nodded. "Like jaundice," he answered.

"Bilious," said the first speaker. "Liver complaint." And he laughed again.

Bert had noticed the man when he came in. He was packing iron, that was certain. He was older than he looked, too, because he sat, steady and calmly, as if there wasn't a nerve in his body. He didn't want people behind him either, because he had rejected the chair offered by the waiter, to sit—like Mel—with his back to the wall. But the old ex-ranger had never seen that good-looking young face before. He puzzled about him, checking again the suspicion that the fellow carried a gun. Nothing else would make that bulge. His flask was on his other hip.

"Haven't I seen you somewhere before?" Mel asked. "Your face is familiar." A stranger with a gun in a land where a king has recently died would bear close scrutiny.

"I don't know. I haven't been here long."

"No. Somewhere else. Chicago, maybe."

The young fellow cast a quick, suspicious glance at Mel. "Maybe."

"No offense. No offense." They drank a moment in silence. "Know anybody out there?"

"Anybody?"

Mel winked.

"No. I'm from Washington."

"Oh—yeah?"

The young man nodded.

"I used to know a fellow from Washington. Had connections there anyway."

"Yes?"

"Name of Shields. Ever hear of Jake Shields?"

"I've read his name in the papers."

"Um—hm. Never met him?"

"Not—lately."

Mel raised his brows. "No—maybe not."

"But I'd like to." The young man's voice was bitter.

"Me too," said Mel and fell to studying the fellow still more minutely. It was all too pat. His old head was immediately wary of a trap. But the case was closed. This chap couldn't be from headquarters. They never went about things in this way. Delicacy— even obtuse delicacy—was beyond them. But the man was not hard. For all his self-assurance, his determined eyes, bitter words and strong chin, he was not tough.

"My liquor's gone," the stranger said a little later. "See you again some time." He rose to go.

"Hold on; I'm leaving too." They went out together. "I'll take you to my favorite saloon," said Mel, thinking that no matter who the man was, he could get away with nothing in Billy's.

Over their drinks at a table in the back room a friendship was formed. Mel was almost convinced that the fellow was on the level. "Just call me 'Benny'; my name's Chase."

"I'm Bert Melcher."

"Yes, I recognized you."

Bert was flattered. "What line?"

Chase shrugged. "What'll turn a penny. I'm not particular."

"Alky?"

"Anything."

"I ain't takin' much interest in my business right now. I'm waitin'. Truth is, things 're uncertain."

"You were Poling's friend."

"I *am* Poling's friend."

"Uh—huh. You want Shields."

"More'n *any*thing."

"Me too. He let me do a stretch for him—in P.A."

"The louse!"

"I want him—badly."

Mel considered once again. He could scarcely imagine this smooth and comely young man who spoke perfect English ever serving time. He would connive some test for him before he gave him his complete confidence.

"I was goin' over to Schneider's later on t'night, jus' to see what I could see."

"That where he got Poling?"

"That's where Poling was got."

"Of course. You're not convinced, then, that Shields did it?"

"I didn't see 'im."

The stranger nodded. "Mind if I go with you?"

There seemed no harm in that, no matter who or what the fellow was. The chance to try him out might turn up. "Let's go."

In Yorkville, to avoid waits for lights, Mel drove tortuously, taking right turns which landed them on a cross-town street some three blocks from the scene of the murder. The street was but dimly lighted and no one moved in the block. As they approached the half-demolished ruins of a recent fire, on their left, a great, gaunt dog loped out of the charred doorway and stood on the curb, his eyes burning on them as they passed the spot without slackening speed. It was a thing seen and—unless coupled with a definite memory—immediately forgotten. They neared the corner before a hazy mental picture occurred to Mel. He saw Slim, dying on a hospital bed, dying for a dog. His brakes burned and he parked quickly on the right, near the corner.

"What's the matter?" Benny asked.

"That's funny."

"What?"

"See 'at dog back there?"

"On the walk? Yes."

"It sure would be funny if that was Old Man Shields' dog."

"He *had* a big dog; but that—'way over here."

"Yeah—but funny things happen. They say his dog jus' hated coppers."

Benny sensed the older man's suspicions. "Let's take a look," he said.

A householder turned the corner, on foot, and glanced at the car before turning up the short steps to his home.

"Oh, friend," Mel accosted him.

The man turned.

"Do you happen to know who owns that dog over yonder?"

"Is he there again? ... No. He's been hangin' around that house for a week or more. Nobody seems to own him. I told the cop about him last night but he didn't do nothin'. Say, he's vicious. He won't let you get near him."

"That so?"

"He's an expensive dog, though."

"I lost one o' them about a week ago. I been lookin' for him."

"Well, he's been around here about a week. If he's yours I guess you're welcome to him. The Goldbergs offered him food one time but he wouldn't touch it."

"Is that so.... Eh—my dog was trained not to eat, except what I gave him.... How long ago was that fire?"

"Two weeks, about—on a Tues—no, a Wednesday—t'day's what? ... Yeah, fourteen, fifteen days ago."

"Thanks."

"O.K.... Don't let 'im bite you."

"No—I don't think he'll bite me."

The man went on into his house, looking back over his shoulder.

The fire had been *two* weeks ago. That would be before the Boss had been killed. The dog had been in the neighborhood about a week. Then he had come since that bloody night.

"C'mon, Chase. Let's see this dog."

They left the car and approached on the sidewalk. The animal had dropped on his belly, his great head resting on his front paws. As the men drew near he lifted a tired nose and regarded them with unmistakable hostility. When they were almost upon him he rose stiffly and growled, showing his teeth, then retreated slowly into the charred basement of the ruin.

Mel was not inclined to talk. It was a long shot. The dog might mean little or nothing. "Wait here," he said and ran back to the car for a flashlight.

"Let's go."

The yellow beam showed them dirty stairs, a smashed door, a dilapidated room with its ceiling falling. Two red spots indicated the wolf-like presence of the dog—in the door beyond.

"Now, listen," said Benny Chase. "If that beast comes at us, is it worth the racket? I'm not goin t' get chewed, but I hate to shoot unless it's necessary."

"Shoot? Hell, no. Get yourself a club."

They looked about for silent weapons of defense. A menacing growl slowed their approach. A foot at a time, armed with heavy sticks, the two men in dinner clothes penetrated deeper and deeper into the dark and menacing place. The dog was cornered. He had backed slowly away from their light and clubs until he reached the back wall of what had been a kitchen. Here, the fire had started. An irregular hole two or three feet across yawned in the floor. A distinct but undefinable odor reached their nostrils through the smell of burned wood.

Despite the growing threat of the beast's louder growl and the still more dangerous fact that he was becoming conscious that he was at bay, hemmed in, Mel threw the flashlight's beam into the basement through the charred hole. As the two men leaned forward to look, the dog sprang, a ravenous catapult of fury. Mel was the nearer. The flashlight shattered. Their clubs were toothpicks. In the dark they were no match for this fiend incarnate who retreated an inch under their blows only to gain a yard at his next onslaught. His flashing teeth and the power of his rushes drove them both from the house. They both bled from arms, hands and face. And still he came on. Mel's test of Benny Chase had meant nothing, or the dog could also smell the taint of the ranger still upon him. They ran for the car, beset by the growling killer who stood on their running board and snapped viciously as Mel started the motor. "I'm—going to—give it to him," Chase stammered, trying to catch his breath.

"Aw right," said Mel. "Now!"

The car leapt forward. A single well-placed bullet dropped the mutt. "Drive like hell," said Benny.

The big Belgian shepherd groveled in the gutter, little clouds of dust rising from his kicking paws.

CHAPTER TWENTY-FOUR

"I'm sorry we had to do that," said Mel. "I know a fellah died for that dog."

"I'm sorry too, Melcher. But, man, look at my hand!"

They drove a few minutes in silence.

"You—you pretty sure that was Shields' dog, are you?" Chase asked.

Mel watched the man's face narrowly. Had he too seen the object in the basement? Half-covered with débris? "I'd bet my last cent," said the westerner.

And Chase wondered if Melcher had had time to see—what *he* had seen—in that brief instant before the dog leaped.

"You hurt bad?" Mel asked.

"Naw. Nothing much. He tore my hand…. Stop at a drug-store, I'll get some iodine."

"You'd bust into a drug-store with blood all over you?"

"It's my own blood."

"Um!" Either this fellow was extremely brave or he was a fool.

"Why not?"

"Risky."

"There's one. Let me out here. I'll walk up an' get it and you can pick me up at the next corner."

"I'll wait outside." The mutual respect of these two men was mounting.

In Schneider's second floor, where the splinters still pointed inward on the door, they applied iodine to their lacerations.

"What do you suppose that mutt wanted to hang around that house for?"

Chase shook his head. "Let me get your ear.... There. Whew, what a mess." He corked the bottle and looked about. "So this is the room. Smelly hole."

"No windows."

"No—good night! And you were here, weren't you?"

"Yeah—I was here."

"Where?"

"In there."

"Oh, not *in* the room?"

"Nope. He was alone when it happened."

"Alone?"

"He was doin' a card trick. I forget how it went now, but each of us took ten cards and left him here, alone.... He and Shields had a bet—five grand on each card. I wisht he had finished the trick. By God, I'll bet he couldn't of done it!"

"Five grand?"

"Yeah—on five cards. That's twenty-five grand Shields stood to lose."

"And you can't remember the trick?"

"Never heard of it b'fore. The Boss kept two cards."

"There must have been five of you then."

"Yeah—they was." Mel's distrust asserted itself again. "Say, Benny. What's the lay? What do you care about this mess? How do I know you ain't a bull?"

"Me—a bull! You know better, Mel. I'm a doctor—in daylight."

"Y' act square, I'll say that. But get this! I'd be willin' to cough up this story to the force, if they wanted it.... So if you want t' go over th' ground, it's nothin' to me."

"Don't be afrai—er—suspicious of me, Melcher. I want to get the fellow we mentioned before. I'd go through hell to get him. I'll be square with you."

Mel looked at the man's jaw where the dog had torn out a piece of flesh and the iodine had mixed with the brilliant red blood, then held out his hand. "It's a go, boy…. Yes, they was five of us."

"Poling was six?"

"Yeah."

"Three besides you and Shields?"

"Right. An' Slim is dead. That leaves two."

"Y' sure it wasn't either one o' them? Zimbronski, maybe?"

"Zim was awfu' drunk an' he'd made a play for the Boss earlier. No. I don't see how it could of been him. They was another fellah with him all the time—in that room."

"In there?"

"Yeah."

"Have you seen either of those men since?"

"I seen Zim on the street. I ain't seen the other one."

"Did you see Zim's gun that night, after the murder?"

"Yes—I—well. Let's see, I ast him for it, but he put me off. But, say, Zim couldn't of done it. Look, there's the bullet holes in the door—an' only Shields went out that way. All the rest of us were on the other side o' the room."

Benny scrutinized the wall opposite the door. "Not a scratch. I figured some of the bullets might have missed him."

"No. Don't try to hang this on Zim. I found Shields' empty gat outside that door when we went out."

"You did?!"

"Sure…. I got it home. A heavy Savage—a special job."

"You—you've still got it?"

"Sure. I almost turned it in once, but the cops didn't want it."

"Yeah, I know. Could I see it, later?"

"I guess so. Why not?"

Benny scrutinized the panel of the door. "Now, where was Poling when you came in?"

"About—there."

"Feet?"

"This way."

"Then he was standing here, with his back to the door. Suppose you stand here—I want to look through the key-hole."

Mel's scalp prickled strangely when the door shut. He reached for his rod, then stayed his hand. That was silly. This fellow was all right-—but he could hardly force himself to take the position in which the Boss must have stood to die as he did.

Finally Chase returned. "Well, I've found *one* thing. The man who shot those holes in the door didn't take aim through the key-hole—because I can't *see* you through the key-hole. You go try it. I'll stand here."

Mel obeyed. "You're right. He must of just shot, blind like, remembering where he was, about, inside."

Benny shook his head. "Maybe he was shooting at something else."

"What do you mean?"

"Maybe someone else was out there, when Shields went out."

"An'—an' they didn't mean to get the Boss? They—might of been shooting at each other?"

"And killed Poling entirely by accident."

"Only one gun went off."

"A knife, perhaps."

"Say! Slim said…. Look here. Only the night before, Shields had killed a Chinaman. Slim told me jus' b'fore he died that maybe they'd followed Shields here. What do you say?"

"It's possible. Now, let's see. How long did it take you to get into the hall, after the shots?"

"Oh, I don't know. We argued. I looked at the Boss. Three—four—five minutes. Lots longer'n I wish it was now, I'll say."

Benny nodded.

"If you had gone there first you would have seen Poling's murderer."

"Sure…. But when we saw the holes, we thought it was Shields."

"Maybe it was."

"An' maybe not."

"When you did get out there, what did you see?"

"Schneider an' a waiter comin' up the steps, with cooks an' bottle washers."

"Were they close to the door?"

"No, oh, no. They were down at the foot o' the steps. Jus' startin' up. Half-way, maybe."

"At least three minutes after the shots were fired?"

"Yeah. Easy."

"Plenty of time had elapsed for—Chinks, let's say—to carry Shields down the steps and out that door?"

"Well, maybe."

"What else? Where was his gun?"

"There. An' the ten cards were scattered, kinda, down here."

"Then you all made a break for it over the roofs?"

"Right."

"Who else had been here that night?"

"Well, friend, I ain't namin' no names, but there was a fellah—an' a girl."

"A girl, eh?"

"A beauty!"

"Know her?"

"Some. The Boss knew 'er. That was all in the papers."

"Yes, I read that. Patsy. And you won't tell me who the man was?"

"Well, he was wanted. He was goin' away. He wouldn't 'a' done it."

"Sure?"

"Well, sure I'm sure."

"Was it this Kid Chilton?"

"Yeah, him."

"He left?"

"Yeah, he beat it."

"How long before the shooting?"

"Oh—ten—fifteen minutes."

"As long as that?"

"About."

"You haven't seen him?"

"Hell, no, he's in Cuba."

"Sure?"

"Well, I been thinkin' so. Maybe not. Jeez, Chase, you sure act like a bull. Ain't you, sure enough?"

Benny shook his head. "No, not me."

"Well, that's all I know. I ain't been doin' much business 'cause I can't get in touch with the proper party on the force an' I'm not doin' anything wholesale until he gets back."

"Who's that?"

"Eh?—Oh, a man."

"Out of town?"

"Yeah. Fishin'."

"I see. He was your protection?"

"He was a friend o' the Boss."

"You never dealt with him?"

"No."

"Did Shields?"

"I guess so."

"So do I."

"We knew we were all O.K. when he said so. But he had a change o' heart that night, on account of that Bronx business."

"You weren't in that, were you, Mel?"

"Nope. That was two other fellahs."

"Had a change of heart, did he?"

"Yeah. He was gonna pinch everybody in town that night."

"Who said so?"

"He did."

"Tell Poling?"

"Eh?—Yes. Sure."

"Well, Mel. Let's go have a look at that gun. Have you handled it much?"

"Not much."

CHAPTER TWENTY-FIVE

Earlier the same evening, Officer Monahan looked in the garage door, next to the hang-out downtown.

"Hullo, Zim. How's thricks?"

"Hello, Pat. How's by you?"

"Nice, Zim. Nice…. I've had advice, Zim, that nobody's to take no cars out ontil Mel sez so."

"Who says so?"

"Mr. Melcher."

"Since when is he Mister to you?"

"Well, it ain't t' be done."

"Well, I'm doin' it."

"No, now, Zim; Mel'll be sore an' jump down me throat. Don't go gettin' me in wrong with y'r new boss."

"Who in hell said Melcher was my new boss? Did *he!*"

"No, I—I don't guess he did. But he *is;* ain't he?"

"He is not. I ain't got no boss. Look out, Pat, I'm comin' out."

"I can't let you, Zim. Mel's told me."

"Get out o' the way, flatfoot." The car moved toward the door.

"Flatfoot, is it. I'll flatfoot you!"

The swarthy gunman drove as if there were no one within a mile. Both wheels crossed Monahan's legs, snapping them. "I told you t' get out o' the way."

The old officer drew and fired for a tire, then fainted from pain and the terrible nausea. The bullet went wild.

Zim drove at a leisurely pace, uptown, through the park, around and about, going—aimlessly—no place. At eight o'clock he ate a bowl of chop suey, and was joined by two nervous young fellows who were ill at ease even in so lowly an environment as a second-floor, second-class, Chinese restaurant. One of them did not even sit down. "Let's blow. Word's aroun' there's a stool out. Nobody knows 'im, nor where 'e is."

"Who says?"

"It came straight. Keep your eye peeled."

"Let's go. We got jus' time t' get there."

Zim drove. At the busy façade of a movie they stopped. The two nervously eager men alighted and bought tickets. Zim took the car twenty feet ahead and drew up without stopping the motor. He opened the back door and tried to make it stay ajar without swinging wide. It was no use. The hinge was weak and would not hold the door at what Zim imagined to be a careless and inconspicuous angle. He put his well-loved automatic on the seat beside him and cocked one knee over it like a broody hen over a chick.

At exactly nine fifteen, the head usher left the treasurer's cage with a heavy bag of cash. He darted swiftly into the foyer under the protecting eye of a uniformed officer who, seeing the cash safely on its way to the manager's office, strolled away to his left.

A nervous black-jack caught the boy behind the ear, not quite on the button. He went down but he was not out. He yelled. Clumsy hands snatched his bag and like a half back with only one man for interference, the two went through the lobby for a long gain. They piled into the rear seat of Zim's car. The clutch responded. They were off at a break-neck speed. Two blocks they made before traffic lights barred further progress, then their chauffeur turned and grinned along the barrel of a regulation service revolver. Their driver was a cop. At the same instant four men—two on each side—stepped on the running boards. "Just hold 'em up a second. This will be painless." The fangs of the two were extracted, fangs in the form of black-jacks and guns. Then the improvised patrol, which had but a moment before been a thieves' conveyance, proceeded to the lock-up.

Zim, thoroughly manacled, stood fuming in a shadow between two detectives, waiting for the wagon. The trick had been neatly turned. Unable to believe his eyes, Zim had looked up from his cigarette into a circle of grim and familiar faces. His beloved automatic had been profaned by the hands of law enforcement, pocketed by an ordinary dick. And he had been forced to give them his cap—to stand and watch an officer take his place at the wheel. With the bracelets securely locked and the business ends of two official revolvers carefully pressing against vital spots in his back, he had been forced to watch the two nervous kids climb into the car, into the maw of the department. Zim took it to heart.

As they jolted to the station, one of his guards asked if he would smoke. "Thanks." A cigarette was lighted in his mouth. But the weed was not a kindness. It was a tongue lubricant. For every man on this duty had heard the tale of genial old Monahan's broken legs. Monahan—who wouldn't hurt a fly.

"This looks like curtains, eh, Zim?"

The little man snorted. "Why 'curtains'?"

"They jus' found out at the bureau that it was you shot Poling."

"Old stuff, bull. Old stuff. Ever'body in town knows I didn't shoot Poling. I wasn't even on the party."

"Anything you'll say may be used against you."

"Well, use this," and he made an English gallery sound with his mouth.

"They jus' found it out t'night. Seems they caught this Patsy woman an' she squawked."

"Aw, go——yourself! I don't know no Patsy woman an' if you caught a dozen you wouldn't have nothin' on me."

"Nothin' on you? Why, Zim, if you was only sentenced one week apiece for every count they got against you—you'd still go up for life."

"Smart cops…. Well, I'm gonna cheat y' out o' your fun t'night. Y' ain't gonna get the chance to pound *me* up. I'm gonna confess."

"*What* 're y' gonna confess?"

"Stealin' rides on taxi-cabs an' throwin' washers in the Salvation Army Christmas kettle. Whadaya think?!"

Big talk continued until the station was reached. Then Zim refused to say another word. They booked him for possession and complicity and put him in a cell. An exceptionally thorough searcher felt the lining of the old coat he wore. In the front corner, below the pocket, he found something stiff. Exploration revealed half of a playing card, dirty and bent.

CHAPTER TWENTY-SIX

There was something wrong at headquarters that night. The louder Zim called for a chance to secure a bondsman, the deafer the law became. No matter how closely he tried to follow Robert's Rules of Order, calling heavily upon his past experience in jail matters to launch his claims at the most politic intervals, he was always out of order, always speaking out of turn. He spat between the bars of his cage and had the trouble of washing it up, just to cool his spleen. Every turnkey and station porter knew that Zim had broken both of Pat Monahan's legs, willfully and intentionally—and that the "Knights of the Rosy Circle" who sat at the head of the department had broken off diplomatic relations with this bit of Polish flotsam. In other words, anything went. Zim was a rat. Bring your poisoned cheese and come over.

He had not yet slept, in his cell across town, as Mel and Benny Chase tried to find finger prints on Shields' gun.

Mel was much the handier at this, although Benny had shown himself a regular butcher, cauterizing those dog bites and bandaging them. Mel shook fine powder from a little pounce and tried to read the result. "There's at least three different ones, but they're pretty old to be much good."

"One of them is yours?"

"Yeah, then two more. I don't know what that proves, exactly."

"Only that someone else has handled the gun besides you and Shields."

"But when? Those prints may be pretty old."

"But not likely."

"Look here, Benny; if you're out to get Shields, it seems damn' funny to me that you're tryin' to make out somebody else fired those shots."

Chase thought very fast. It was becoming more and more necessary to think fast and faster around this tall man from Texas. "I told you I was a doctor, part time, Mel. I guess it's the scientist in me that keeps digging at the truth of the matter regardless of how much I'd like to hang it on Shields."

"Oh, forget science. Jake Shields done it all right."

"Have you anything else against the man—if it was proved that he didn't kill Poling?"

"No! But, Jesus, Benny, don't try to hang this thing on half o' Chinatown. I don't want to start no yellow pogrom…. Not by myself."

Mel's 'phone rang.

"There's a stool out, Mel. Thought I'd tip you. They got Zim."

"Whadayamean 'got'?"

"In the can."

"What charge?"

"Tryin' t' stick up a movie with two other guys."

"What about this other?"

"Y' mean the pigeon?"

"Yeah."

"Nobody knows much. It's jus' goin' aroun' that one is workin'. I'd watch my step."

"Thanks."

As the receiver slipped back into place, Mel's thin lips were drawn under his gray mustache. He turned to look into the muzzle of a large caliber Colt's. "Your friend talks too loud, Mel. And I'm sorry you have such a suspicious disposition. I never meant you the least harm and I'm not a stool pigeon. But I don't stand a chance with you if you think I am. I'm taking Shields' gun and I'm leaving. You stay here."

"Sonny, put up your toy. I ain't half so suspicious as I look. You an' me has fought wolves t'gether. Put it up."

Benny shook his head. "No, Mel. I can't risk it. I've got to get out of here right away. You just sit still."

The ex-ranger had made no move to raise his hands. They lay on top of the table just as they were when he hung up the telephone. A slow grin spread across his face and his eyes were amused. "W'y, Bennie," he drawled, squinting up at the young fellow who had him covered, "ef I was t' draw now—or maybe lunge at y'—I'm doubtin' if you'd shoot."

"Don't try it, Mel. It hurt me to shoot that dog. It'd almost kill me to shoot you, but I'd do it if I had to."

Mel shook his head and rose, heedless of the other's revolver. "Y' ain't gonna haf to, son. Take his gun an' run along. It don't mean a damn' thing t' me. If you're goin' back to the station, ride with me; I'm goin' down an' see if I can do anything for Zim. They just took him in."

Benny was wrapping Shields' gun clumsily in a handkerchief with his one free hand. "I'm not going to the station. I'm not a cop." Then he backed to the door. "Good-night, Mel."

"Good-night, son. Good luck."

The door closed.

CHAPTER TWENTY-SEVEN

The papers made a great fuss about Zim's capture. They also chronicled the return to the city of Deputy Commissioner Martin. Now things would hum. "Eyewitness Martin", the noblest evidence-getter of them all, was back in the saddle. Zim didn't have a chance. They had his gun. They had half a card from the broken deck in the Poling case. They had his hat and shoes from the Bronx massacre. Zim was as good as dead.

Much was made of the torn card. It was like a movie plot. The edges fitted exactly into those of half a card found the night of the murder. The newspapers tortured that fact into all but an admission of guilt. Then three whole cards from the same deck arrived in the mail, each addressed to a different member of the force. Martin received one. Carl Denby received one. Another detective got the third.

The next day came three more. They were all turned over to Denby who had inherited those McQuirk had collected when he took over the job.

"Zim claims he burned nine of them. If he's tellin' the truth, that leaves only four more." Every effort was bent upon locating the man who was mailing the cards.

Despite the collapse of the card evidence, despite the District Attorney's almost air-tight case against Zim for the Bronx affair, nothing happened. The District Attorney and Carl Denby talked it over.

"They want me to burn him for Poling; can you imagine that? They want me—*and* you—to get evidence against Zim for killing Poling."

"He never done it."

"Me neither—but that's the word."

"I can't do it. It means fixed witnesses, a hung jury, God knows what all. I can't frame that."

"Tell him so."

"I told him."

"What'd he say?"

"Say? He says, 'You do it or I'll put somebody in there who can.' That's what he said."

"I'm going to fight him, Carl. He can't hurt me. I'm going to indict Zim tomorrow for murderin' those cops in the Bronx.... Somebody must be payin' a pretty penny for this Poling job. Who d' you think it is?"

"Shields."

"I wouldn't doubt it. An' if Zim could burn for it, Old Man Shields'd sleep better nights. Ain't that a mess?"

CHAPTER TWENTY-EIGHT

hen there came, to block and forestall the ends of justice, the greatest mass of legal technicalities and red tape ever centered on a single criminal case. There were writs and delays and contested verdicts. There were charges of corruption, appeals, more writs, accusations, perjury, counter-charges. Witnesses were incompetent. Zim was insane. Delay—delay—delay. But in spite of all the legal chicanery and skill that were brought to bear, it could not be erased from the minds of the jury-men that this little, sharp-featured Pole had turned his gun on American defenders of the peace—and shot them down from behind.

They called him "guilty," and the judge sentenced him to be electrocuted at such and such a time in the future.

The furor started again. Appeal—appeal—appeal. Then, finally, stay of execution, stay of execution, stay of execution. From week to week his life was spared. From month to month he lingered on in his cell, held back from the death house by some power no man could see. Kept from paying the penalty his deeds demanded, by the strong but invisible arm of some potentate who wanted him to live.

To his cell they brought an envelope, containing another of those playing cards in which McQuirk had once placed so much faith. It had been scrutinized and photographed carefully before they gave it to him. He just grinned. "You'd like t' know where those are comin' from; wouldn't you?"

"*You* don't know."

"Oh, yes, I do. But why tell you? It won't get me nothin'."

"It might."

"What'll it get me?"

"If you's to get religion an' tell who killed Poling—it might get you a commutation."

"Nothin' doin'. Make it a pardon or nothin'."

"The Governor can't pardon *you*. The public'd lynch him. Ain't you got no idea how they hate you? Don't you know how rotten you are?"

"Then why don't they bump me off? I ain't askin' for all these stays. I'd a lot rather have it done. I been ready a long time."

"Everybody ain't so ready. C'mon. Where the cards comin' from? I swear you'll get life instead o' the chair if you'll do what I say."

"Nope. Your oath ain't no better than my word."

"Then you'll burn—in a week."

"Why not tonight? I ain't got nothin' to do."

CHAPTER TWENTY-NINE

Meanwhile, through all the weary months of the trial, McQuirk had been at work. First, Benny Chase had reported back to him—with Shields' gun and the story of the dog. Together they had gone over every step of the crime, piecing together the fragments, trying to fit the girl Patsy into the tale. Trying to learn her whereabouts.

"As we leaned over that hole, just before the dog jumped, I thought I saw a foot—in the basement."

"What?" McQuirk left his chair. "*Thought* you saw a foot? Let's go."

"We better wait 'til dark. We don't want to attract attention."

"You're right.... But a *foot!* A foot means a body, Benny. And a body—"

A calendar was found—and the date of the fire marked. "How long could a body lay there like that without attractin' attention?"

"Under cover of the burned wood and smoke smell—a long time."

"It wouldn't be the body of somebody in the house when it burned. The firemen or the insurance boys would of found it. It's been put there since."

"I figured that."

"Ten to one it's an old shoe!"

"Maybe."

They returned to their scrutiny of the fingerprints taken from Shields' gun.

"One set is Melcher's. One is Shields'—an' one is …"

"The man that got Poling."

"Benny—I believe you're right."

"But, Mac; how are we going to tell them apart?"

"I'd know Mel's with my eyes shut. I've seen 'em a thousand times."

"But Shields'? The cops won't let us see them."

"Benny…. We'll get Shields's off of Shields—if it ever gets dark. That dog wasn't wastin' his life away for no tramp."

"You mean, he's been in that cellar—ever since that night?"

"I'll bet my share of Kingdom Come that's right where he's been. If you saw a foot—it was Shields' foot. If all you seen was a shoe—it was Shields' shoe. I know dogs."

They waited until their patience was burned out, trying to hold their curiosity until that street would be quiet. Finally, before eleven, they drove to the spot where Chase had shot the dog, then on into the next block. Discovery would be uncomfortable; it might spoil their whole plan. They left the car and returned singly, on foot. Benny went in first, and waited at the door for McQuirk.

Nothing had been changed. There were the bloody clubs they had dropped, there the broken door and sagging ceiling. They went softly, throwing twin beams of light ahead of their feet. Their pulses were high. Despite their professions, surgeon and man-hunter, these two were not normal, could not bid their nerves and hearts be normal under these circumstances. They hoped to learn something momentous, but it involved finding a corpse—and that alone was bad enough. Besides, there was something ominous in the stillness of the place, as if something living and not dead waited to pounce upon them.

"I—I wonder if I actually killed that dog," Chase whispered. "Maybe he crawled back in here."

"Sh-sh-sh."

They entered the kitchen. McQuirk had advised that they come unarmed, since he had relinquished his right to that precaution and Benny had never had it. Now, both wished they had been less meticulous. A pistol is a great strengthener of spirit in a strange, dark, cellar near midnight—even in the presence of the dead. The odor Benny had noticed the night before had noticeably increased.

Their flashlights found the charred hole and they craned their necks to see—

"Stick 'em up!" A hard round object pressed into the ribs of each man, from behind. "Higher! Now, turn out them lights." They obeyed.

It was the police!

No!

The police would not have made them turn out their lights. A bright beam of a third lamp blinded them, then a heavy hand holding a revolver shoved itself into the beam. "Back up! ... Now, what do you want in here?" Both men were too shaken to identify the voice. They answered not a word but tried hard to see into the blackness beyond that gun.

"How come you two are trainin' together? What's the racket?"

"Why, why, it's ..."

"Never mind who it is! What 're you two doin' in here—an' why together?"

"I thought I saw something down there last night," said Benny. "We came back to see."

"I thought you was off the force, McQuirk."

"I am. This—this is a private enterprise. Me an' Chase 're workin' for Lloyd's o' London.... Shields carried big insurance with 'em an' they won't pay it until it's proven he's dead."

Melcher was silent. It sounded reasonable. McQuirk had always been a square shooter. "Turn around." He went over them for irons, then put his own away. "All right. I don't believe a damn word of it. Put down your hands. Light up, if you like. I'm tossin' in with you."

"Great!" Chase ejaculated.

McQuirk extended his hand. "Let's shake, Mel. Honest, this ain't for the bureau."

"I b'lieve y'—an' I like this punk here. Where'd y' pick 'im up?"

"He ain't so young. He's a damn good doctor."

"Well, let's see what's in the cellar."

Three beams explored the darkness through the hole in the floor. The foot was found, an arm protruded and one side of the head. An inefficient attempt had been made to cover the body with débris.

"It's him," said Mel. "He had on them gaiters that night. I remember."

They paused for a council. What did any or all of them know about that? How had he got there? Who had done it? When?

"He's been dead at least a week," said Benny. "I can see that from here."

Melcher wrinkled his nose. "Cheeze," he said, "I'd hate to be a doctor."

McQuirk's analytical mind was leaping ahead of them. "No woman ever carried that heavyweight down Snider's steps and over here. That'd take a man. Maybe more'n one."

"They must of had a car. They'd 'a' been stopped otherwise. That time. People passin' all the time."

"Maybe he ran in here to hide, and got it here. Fell down that hole in the dark an' broke his neck…. Maybe he was wounded and hid in there, and died later."

"I'll tell you more about that when I look at him," said Benny. "I can tell you what killed him."

"Who tried to cover him up, then, if he died in here?"

"The dog—maybe."

"Maybe. Your guess is as good as mine. Shall we go down there an' look him over?"

"How about the police?"

McQuirk's brows met in a troubled frown. But he hesitated only a second. "Never mind them. We found 'im. Let's go."

They worked with the utmost caution—in defiance of the law. Urged on by a duty they esteemed more highly than subservience to a farcical misapplication of justice, they took the investigation of this case into their own hands and applied their combined talents to its solution.

They had not come prepared to work that first night, but they came again and again, slipping into the ruin one at a time, laden with paraphernalia, with cameras, plates and surgical instruments. The need for quiet and absolute secrecy slowed their work, but at length it was done. They had photographed everything: the floors, the cellar, the body before they touched it. They took the fingerprints of the dead hands and made enlargements of prints they found on the face. While Melcher and McQuirk held powerful auto-lanterns, Doc Chase probed two leaden pellets from the man's head. Then, one at a time, they slipped quietly out of the place. McQuirk carried the largest roll of banknotes he had ever seen.

On the third day after the discovery of the body, the old detective sent an anonymous letter to his former assistant, Carl Denby, taking every precaution to avoid pitfalls which might lead to his identification. The letter read: "Body in cellar burnt house 80 Street."

CHAPTER THIRTY

The police had taken the body without letting the reporters in on it. They had accepted its mutilated condition in stoic amazement, revealing none of their thoughts. A coroner's physician had seen at a glance that the body had been handled recently, that the probing had been done long after death. The department was wary of a trap and two men were put on the trail of McQuirk's letter. Something they had not suspected was going on under cover. But what? It had hastened Zim's trial for the moment. It had brought about the order to pin the Poling job on him. It had cost him a night's sleep—a hellish night of questions he could not answer.

The papers had finally been permitted to announce that gangland had taken its own toll. That Poling was avenged. The *Register*, to avoid drawing attention to itself, had printed an outline of the same story, committing itself to nothing. The time was not yet ripe for the true story. They needed a few more facts.

Then it had been forgotten in the glory of Commissioner Martin's successful accumulation of evidence that was to send Zim to the chair. But Zim saw no hope of the end—not yet. His hair had grayed, his face grown haggard. He came to look like a patriarchal rat.

Then the patience of all concerned wore thin and thinner. His last stay, his last reprieve, respite and delay had been granted. There would be no more. There *could* be no more. At twelve-fifteen *tonight*. The arrangements were made. The invitations sent out. The Governor fled to an unknown retreat. Nothing could stop it now. *Nothing!*

Then, at eleven—or a few minutes after—the warden was found by a liveried chauffeur. He was followed by a veiled woman, gorgeously gowned and swathed in the rarest furs, the softest, richest satins. The chauffeur tendered her credentials and the lady was taken to the death house. Last-minute badinage, hard-boiled farewells few men have ever heard, greeted her ears. She stood before Zim's cell and lifted her veil.

"Patsy!"

PART FOUR

CHAPTER THIRTY-ONE

The mysterious woman dropped her veil at once. "Not so loud, Zim. I can't be arrested now. I've been through too much."

"*You* been through!"

"Oh, I know—"

"What about me?"

"Zim, I had to see you."

"You waited long enough."

"Zim! Every stay you got—"

"I see. Through you, eh? Doin' me favors…. Thanks!"

"Zim, I've got to know. Did he get away?"

"Did who get away?"

"Where is he?"

"Who do you mean?"

"The—the Kid."

"The Kid." Zim snorted. "Why shouldn't he? What'd he do? Have you come here to tell me *now* that he got the Boss?"

"No, no. You know better. But I haven't had a line; not a word. I can't go on unless he's safe. I can't."

The death house had become mysteriously, ominously silent. These two had an audience of at least six interested men. Those who could not hear were quiet, biding their time. This would make tomorrow pass the quicker. It would give them something to talk about. Most of the condemned men understood at least a portion of the whispered tableau.

"I don't know a thing," said Zim. "Not a thing."

"Ain't you heard from him?"

He did not answer. "Where you been, Patsy? Where'd you get the clothes? It don't look to me like you was sufferin' much."

"Don't say that, Zim. I've been through hell."

"You know who got the Boss. I'm a dead man, Pat. I'll trade with you. Tell me you'll see that he gets his—an' I'll tell you what I know."

The warden and the chaplain followed the turn-key toward them along the corridor.

"They're coming, Zim. Quick. I promise. I'll see that he gets it. I'll do it. Is the Kid all right?"

"Sure he is. Safe as a church. Now, who was it got Poling? … You promised."

"Where is the Kid?"

"Who was it?"

The little group stopped. "You will have to go, madame, unless you wish to watch the—eh—"

"No—oh, God, no!" Patsy shrank back.

"That guard will let you out."

She took two steps away. "Come back here," Zim yelled. "Come back an' keep your promise. You can't run out like that…. You little tramp! Come back." They tried to silence him. The other inmates began to murmur and mock his voice. Zim continued to scream. "You can't let her go. She's as guilty as I am. That's Patsy. That's the woman in the Poling case…. She knows who killed him. She killed 'im 'erself. Y' can't let *her* go—an' kill me!"

Patsy continued her half-blind progress toward the grated door which led to the open air and freedom.

"D' ya call this justice, you hounds? Are y' gonna let 'er go? Open this door, I'll get 'er. I'll kill 'er. Let me out!"

Patsy's slim form, set off for the first time in raiment suitable to its grace and elegance, disappeared from view.

"Shut up, now, Zim. That lady had a pass t' see you. Y' ought to be glad she came."

"Glad, yeah; I'm glad. You dogs, you filthy, low-down skunks! You're gonna burn *me*, but you let her go b'cause she's got a pass. How'd she get it, huh? How'd she get 'er pass? It's too damn bad I ain't a woman. I wouldn't burn either. I'd go out an' eat chicken an' go to a show—like her. No matter how many men I'd killed. But I'm a man."

"You're a worm," said his next cell-mate. "Go sit down on the hot spot an' quit bellyachin'."

"I'll keep it warm for you, y' bastard."

And thus he went out, loudly, blasphemously, bitterly. He cursed and accused his jailers, he screamed highly colored phrases at the witnesses and the reporters as he was strapped in the chair.

Guy Field did not wait for the switch to be thrown that would send this screeching madman to another hell. From this word and that phrase, which his fellow reporters tried to catch in shorthand for the business of spicing their stories in the papers, Guy pieced together a fact that was slower to occur to them. Patsy Shelling had been in the death house—only a moment before. That meant that even now, she was driving away—or going to the depot. He bolted for the door. It was no uncommon sight to the guard. Many a man who could cross the roughest sea had no stomach for a spectacle like this. He opened the door quickly and Guy ran to the next iron-barred gate.

"In there," said that man.

"No, not that. I want to get out. I've got to get out, quick."

"Let's see your card."

Guy found it—and was released. One more door. "Did a lady just leave?"

"Yeah. She's just goin'."

A beautiful brown and gray limousine was circling the gravel road, heading back to New York. "Class," said Guy to himself, "heavy class. Gosh, this is a break." Three cabs were parked, but no drivers were in sight. Where the devil were they? Inside. Watching the electrocution or shooting craps. No time. He jumped to the seat of one taxi and turned the engine over. Luck was with him. There was no locking device in place. He was off.

He kept the big car in sight most of the way to town. When it escaped him he drove frantically until he found it again. On Riverside Drive it stopped. While she gave her chauffeur instructions, Guy approached the apartment house door on foot.

Patsy looked at him sharply as he held the door open for her, then passed in with a murmured "thank you". The night attendant assumed they were together. Patsy assumed the young man lived in the building, or was calling on someone who did.

They left the elevator at the same floor. The car descended. Guy's trained mind had worked fast. One couldn't follow rules in his business. Circumstances made new rules necessary every few minutes, sometimes every few seconds. He had come thus far with this girl because her chauffeur and the building's attendants could not be expected to talk. If this were Patsy Shelling, she was hiding here, albeit a little openly, and they would all protect her; were all warned to protect her. She would have an assumed name and it would be a long, hard job to ascertain that name. But—at her apartment door, he could learn the number; that would make it simpler.

He pretended to be looking for someone, surreptitiously watching her. As she unlocked her door with her key he would approach, and insinuate his foot before she could close it. "Beg pardon, Miss Shelling. May I speak to you a moment," he would say.

But Patsy fooled him. She had no need for a key. She did not even turn the knob. Someone within swung the door wide for her and it was closed before Guy could reach it. 5 B. Well, that was something. Maybe he was better off—knowing that without alarming her.

To attract as little attention as possible, he walked down the steps, and when a good opportunity afforded, slipped quietly to the street. His cab was still waiting. Guy debated. Leave it? No, that would be a tip-off in the morning when the theft got out. He drove for twelve blocks, ignoring the hails of possible fares, and parked again. Then, thoughtfully, he scrubbed at the wheel and control handles with his handkerchief. There would be no fingerprints for the bureau to ponder. Then he called McQuirk.

CHAPTER THIRTY-TWO

The District Attorney was well pleased with himself. He could hear Albany calling. He had convicted and electrocuted one of the toughest gangsters in the East, a man who had been given police protection for years, in spite of his bloody hands. A show-down was coming and the lawyer welcomed it. The city was not big enough to hold both Martin and him. When the volcano finally erupted, he meant to be on top. But when could he force the eruption? All the dope-running and bootlegging millions were back of the crook. And how money talked. How it had slowed up his prosecution of Zim. At times he had been almost beaten. Almost ready to quit.

Martin was funny. First he stopped the boys from looking for a man—Poling's killer, for instance. Then, when they had a tough gunman who hadn't a leg to stand on in public opinion, he tried to railroad him for the crime. Even when there were a score of other counts that would send the fellow up. Then he tried every way in the world to save the man's worthless life—and ended by clamping the lid back on and forbidding further investigation of the Poling case.

It was all too thick. What was the next move? Who was still at large who could help him? Melcher? That other man of Shields'? Who was that guy? Nobody seemed to pay much attention to him. But he had been on the spot. He had seen everything. If he could be located, and treated on the side, maybe Martin could be forced to a show-down.

Where were those playing cards coming from? Were they really important? The case was over a year old. The trail was cold. There were three cards needed to complete the deck. Were Chilton and Patsy in Cuba?

There was another case, strangely quiet. Brown, and what's-his-name, a detective. Two men killed in a gambling-house brawl, and nothing had been done about it. The gambling money was back of Martin too. All of the hundreds of illicit millions made by organized crime were holding that man upright in a throne that sat on the rottenest of foundations. Could he trick Chilton or the girl into returning to the United States? Could he *find* them? Nor was money all. There was an army of sharp-shooting thugs at the man's beck and call. He was protected like an Oriental rajah. He lived like an heir to a throne.

Oh, for one loop-hole. For just one crack in his armor! At first it had seemed to be Shields who guided those puffy fingers. But Shields was dead. Another murder without an arrest. Who had killed Old Man Shields? Melcher? Zim? Melcher could be seen every other day on Broadway. He, apparently, had nothing to hide. Who was that other duck?

Who were the king pins, now that Poling and Shields were both gone? Melcher didn't seem to be doing much of anything, running around with a young fellow who looked honest enough. This other lad?

He called Carl Denby on the phone, "I've been worrying about those cards, Carl. You know?"

"What cards?"

"Those cards you got through the mail, playing cards."

"Oh, them."

"Yes…. Where'd they come from, Carl?"

"Well, I don't exactly know. I wish I did."

"Have you received any more?"

"No. I got almost a deck now, countin' the torn ones."

"You need three more, don't you?"

"Wait a minute…. Yes, three."

"You got the envelopes?"

"Yes."

"Can I see 'em? … I'll come over."

"Aw right. But don't say nothin' about it. I don't think the big fellow'd like it."

"Mum's the word. I'll be right over."

As they studied the envelopes, the attorney told Denby that he had a poison pen case that worried him and he was looking for similar clews. "Just let me borrow these, Carl. I'll return them."

"The big boy'd kill me."

"He won't know."

"He knows *every*thing."

"Just for a few days. I'll not say a word."

"Well, it's up to you. If I get in a jam, you'll have to help me out."

One of the envelopes was postmarked from Newark, N. J. Attorney Frisbee despatched it, just as it had come in, to detective headquarters there—where Martin's power was not so marked. A polite note on the stationery of the District Attorney asked that its sender be located, if possible.

CHAPTER THIRTY-THREE

M elcher, McQuirk, Chase and Guy Field held a consultation of war. All of the morning papers had carried the story of Zim's execution, all mentioned the visit of a mysterious veiled lady whose name could not be learned. What lacings those reporters had taken in their respective offices. What names they had been called. The animal kingdom had been ransacked for stupid mammals with which to compare their mentalities.

In another place, in each paper, as an entirely unconnected incident, the mad prank of one reporter, unnamed, was described as a serious offense. Reporters were sometimes hoodlums, even vandals, that was known. But this latest escapade of one of them was a very grave offense and it was thought that the taxicab line would ask for his arrest. He had, the story said, stolen a march on his friends in the execution chamber and had driven back to the city in a cab chartered by a group to cover the electrocution of Zimbronski.

The cab had been found in good condition but almost empty of gas. If an example were made of this young scape-grace it might tend to reduce complaints in the future.

Only one editor had been astute enough to see the connection between the stolen cab and the mysterious lady.

"See," he had hissed at his own man on the case. "There's a reporter. *He* followed her! He had to steal a cab to do it—but he followed her. While you sat there satisfying a sadistic tendency that is the bane of the human race."

"If he followed her why didn't they spring the story? There's nothin' much in the *Register* that I can find."

"I'll bet you ten dollars they know who that woman was."

"Then why don't they spring it? There's six million people in this town and every damn' one of 'em wants to know."

"Well—why didn't you steal a car and chase her? He tried, anyway." But that was all in the privacy of the office. In McQuirk's home the miscreant listened to McQuirk's analysis of their case.

"We've got to make her *talk!* Get me, *talk!*"

"How you gonna make her talk, Mac? We ain't the law. She don't have to talk, an' from what the boy says she's so well fixed she won't want to talk."

"Didn't get her name?"

"No, but the license number is 006-338. We can find out who owns that. And she lives in 5 B."

"She's the key. Her story is all we need."

"What do you suppose she wanted with Zim?" McQuirk asked.

"Zim'd met her," Mel answered. "But I don't know what she went out there for. It's beyond me."

"If we could only get her tip on who else was on those stairs ... Y' know, she must 'a' been an eye witness, if that slob of a dishwasher knew what he saw," said McQuirk.

"She was more than an eye witness," said Guy. "She's got brains. I'll bet she was in on the whole thing."

"Well, she wasn't alone. She couldn't have taken Shields' gun away from him. Those fingerprints are a *man's*. She couldn't have moved the body. Nope. She's a witness, that's all."

"You sure it was bullets from his own gun that killed Shields?" Mel asked.

"Absolute."

"Our case is open and shut. All we need is her story," Benny Chase said.

"Why not frame her? We know where she lives. We can get the name she uses. Why not get her friend Dolly to call her up—or call on her?"

"There's a thought. Maybe we can talk her out of it."

Mel had been trying to recall something. "Say, y' know who's keepin' her? … Happy!"

Everyone was silent for a moment. It had been so obvious no one had thought of it. They had overlooked the forest, scrutinizing the trees.

"That's how she got into the death house last night."

"That's why she's been so quiet."

"And that's why she won't talk now."

"Won't talk! Won't talk! My dear boy she don't have to talk. If Happy Martin is payin' her bills we can spill the whole thing in the papers. Sock him with a charge of—of, why, we'll make him an accessory after the fact and put 'em both on the witness stand."

But Chase was not so enthusiastic. "Wait a minute, Mac. We've got to prove that Martin is—er—keeping her. That won't be easy. Then we'll have to prove—no, that's too uncertain. That comes down to a dish-washer's word against hers. That won't do."

"How come you thought of Happy, Mel?"

"The night it happened, when she come in, she said she'd been with him all afternoon. She tipped us off that he was goin' to make some pinches—an' maybe stop Shields' boat from going out."

"Yeah?"

"Sure. I'll bet she bought Happy off by—by goin' to him."

"Y' mean—she's doin' this for Kid Chilton? She's so stuck on the Kid that she'd do *that* for him?"

"Right."

"My God! That must be this—whatd'ya call it—love?"

Benny Chase was impressed. "I'd like to meet a woman who would do that for the man she loved."

McQuirk was weighing human nature. "Look! If that's the straight of this, she hates Happy. If we show her how to break him—she'll train with us."

"Let's get Dolly. That'd crack the ice. I think this's got to be handled kinda easy."

"Gently does it," said Chase. "I agree. Let's start with Dolly. Who knows where she lives?"

"That's easy. What then?"

"I don't know, but I'm glad I didn't kill either one of those two men. The man who did is getting closer to his last day every minute now. How about it, Mac?"

"Huh! I'm glad I'm not Happy Martin. That's the boy I'm glad I'm not. Because *he's* gettin' closer an' closer to an awful bust in the nose."

CHAPTER THIRTY-FOUR

The head of Newark's detectives had been fledged beneath McQuirk's heavy wing. Many times in the course of his present incumbency he had called upon bis mentor for advice. The request of the New York District Attorney had seemed a little unreasonable to him. He was asked to locate the sender of a single letter. He had only one envelope and a single playing card from which to start. He learned when and where it had been mailed and there his information stopped. He pocketed the envelope and drove to the city, to McQuirk's home. Mac and Guy Field were alone.

"Well, I'll be damned! Hello, Chuck! Glad t' see you. Come in, boy…. Guy, this is Charley Phillips, from Newark. Guy's on the *Register*."

"Good-evening…. That's the only decent paper in your whole blamed town."

"That's what I've been telling Mac," Guy laughed. "But he wasn't impressed."

"He wouldn't admit it if he was. Mac's a chronic grouch."

"Grouch, eh?" the old detective grinned. "Listen. You come at a peach of a time to eat those words. Guy an' me are waitin' here for a girl—"

"Oh, he's not grouchy around the ladies—I didn't mean that."

"Shut up! This girl is comin' on business."

"Monkey business!"

"Not on your life. Get this, Chuck. We've got Dolly Cushing on her way up here with two of our men."

"I thought you was off the force."

The men found chairs in the comfortable old living-room and lit their cigarettes.

"I am…. But I ain't dead yet. I'm workin' on a murder."

Phillips was surprised. "Yeah? Which one? Who's dead?"

"Clyde Poling."

"Poling! … Why, he's been dead over a year!"

"Nobody's ever been tried for it."

"I know, but—why don't you get a nice fresh case? Why work on one that ain't supposed to be mentioned in our better circles?"

"That's why we're workin' on it, Chuck. We think it ought to be mentioned in our better circles. We think somebody ought to burn for it."

"But how come? Where do you fit? The heirs?"

"Heirs! There ain't any heirs. We're heir to the grief, that's all."

"Who's the girl?"

"She was Poling's sweetheart."

"Oh, yes, I remember, plump blonde."

"That's her."

"She important?"

"We're gonna use her…. We've found Patsy—the only person in the world, I guess, who knows who did it."

"Is that a fact?"

"You remember!"

"Well, it's been a long time…. Who'd you say is bringin' her?"

"Two fellows. Bert Melcher and a friend of ours—doctor. Cousin o' yours, ain't he, Guy?"

"Yes, Benny Chase, my cousin."

"All you fellows workin' on a year-old case?" The Newark man burst out laughing. "Oh, boy, that's funny! Ha-ha-ha-ha! An' I'll bet the office don't even know you're doing it."

"They don't! But I don't see what's so funny about it. What've you got that you're so proud of? Some flimsy little old case anybody could work out. Comin' over here to me to do your work for you.... C'mon, out with it. A mysterious letter, I'll bet a dollar."

Phillips grinned. "Well, it's a mysterious letter—or envelope, all right. You got that much straight. But it ain't dated 1902!"

"Let's see it. You never will be a detective, so help me."

Charley tossed an envelope on the table. "There you are. Open it carefully, look it over—an' tell me who sent it."

McQuirk opened the flap of the large envelope gingerlyand with mock solemnity removed the smaller one, addressed to *Carl Denby, New York Police Department.* He looked back at his pro- tégé. "Where'd you get this?"

"Frisbee sent it over from the District Attorney's office. It was mailed from Newark."

"Yeah, I see." His fingers found the playing card and he held it a moment under the light. Then his laughter bellowed and rocked the pictures on the walls. "Oh, boy!" he roared, "Ooooh, that's hot." Gales and peals of laughter shook his heavy frame until finally it was noticeable to the sleuth from Newark that the laughter was being forced. It was not spon- taneous and hearty as it had been at first; it was—in short—a horse laugh.

"Well, well, what's it all about? Let us in on it."

"Oh, oh, oh, oh, Mamma! This is rich. Look, Guy, this bird is razzin' us for workin' on an old case ! Why, you poor dodo, this is one o' the cards from the room where Poling was murdered. You're workin' on the same case yourself!"

When the three had laughed the humor out of the situation, Chuck returned to his original demand. "All right. I'm the goat. But who mailed it?"

"I'll tell you that too, boy. A fellow named Al Turner mailed that card—and a lot more like 'em. He's the only man that's got any of the deck left an' he's a hop-head. He started mailin' 'em when Zim was pinched—months ago—an' it was the only thing that kept Zim from bein' tried for killing his own boss."

"Honest?"

"Sure. They wanted to hang that thing on Zim—an' might of railroaded 'im for it, usin' a half of one o' these cards for evidence. Then a stream of 'em began comin' in—an' made the force a monkey."

"You know this fellow, this Turner?"

"Sure! But he's nuts. He's harmless…. You know what I mean. He packs a rod an' shoots a little now an' then, but not very straight. He was in the room with Zim the night Poling was killed. He took ten o' these cards away with him."

"Well, I'm a donkey's uncle…. Say, Mac, let me spring this on Frisbee myself, will you? It'll make him look cheap. I know he thinks I can't find the man…. We'll tell him later how I found out, but just for now …"

The door-bell interrupted him. "There they are…. Sure. It's O.K. with me. Don't tell him where you got it…. Here, put it away, and for heaven's sake don't scare this girl. We *need* her."

Mel and Benny ushered Dolly into the room. "Good evening, Mr. McQuirk," she said. She cast a somewhat furtive look at the other two men, then up at Melcher, who reassured her.

"It's all right, Dolly. Set down."

McQuirk hastened to show her a chair.

"Hello, Mel," Phillips greeted. "Since when have you taken up with the flatfeet?"

"Well, I'll tell you, Chuck. When there's guys like you an' Mac here to do business with, I'd jus' as soon be a cop myself. But take 'em all—by an' large, ragtag an' bob-tail—they're a lousy—beg pardon, Dolly—they're a bum bunch."

"Especially some of them," Chuck helped him out.

"Yeah, you're right. Most especially *some* of 'em."

"Well, Dolly," said Mac, "we've found Patsy."

"Yes.... This, this gentleman told me," nodding toward Benny. "She didn't do it, did she, Mr. McQuirk?"

"Well, I hardly think so, Dolly. It don't seem likely. You wouldn't say Patsy could take a man's gun away from him, kill him, carry his—say, nearly two hundred pounds—down a flight of steps, drag it nearly four blocks before one o'clock at night and throw it in ..."

"No, no, of course not. But who are you talking about? Clyde was ..."

"Oh, Shields, my dear! Shields. He was found, you know, shot with his own gun."

"No, she couldn't do that."

"Well, then, I guess she couldn't have killed Poling, because that's what happened.... But, Dolly, Patsy knows who did do it, and we want her to tell us."

"You want me to go and ask her?"

"Well, we wanted you to get her to talk to us. You see, Patsy is—er—very well fixed, now. She's living in a fine apartment, has piles of clothes and jewelry, a car and a chauffeur and a maid.... She's changed a lot. Maybe she won't want to tell us.... Do you think you could get it out of her?"

"Is she with that Happy?"

"I'm afraid so."

"Oh, gosh! Poor Patsy.... Sure, she'll talk to me.... How she hates that man! Any man with a stomach like that." She glanced hastily around the room to see if she had offended anyone present. "You—you all mustn't think—too—too bad about Patsy—for that. She don't want to live with him. It—it was part of the agreement, so the Kid could get away…. That was, besides all the money Clyde gave Happy."

Mac put his palm to his forehead. "Oh, my sacred aunt, if we could only prove *half* of this…. Go on, Dolly, go *on!*"

The girl smiled timidly. "That's all I know. She used to cry herself to sleep, she wanted to do something for the Kid so bad. He never knew she was goin' to Happy as soon as he was on the boat. She was supposed to follow him to Cuba, but something happened. She made me swear never to tell, but I'm tired of waiting for the police to get the man that killed—Clyde…. I'll do anything I can to help."

"You're going to do it, Dolly. We need you. Now, how do you think Patsy will take it best? We mustn't frighten her. She's probably afraid of Happy. Afraid he'll do something terrible if she talks."

"Ye-e-es. If she wasn't afraid, she'd have followed George. I know she would. They wanted to get married."

"Hasn't she ever written to you or called—in all this time?"

"No, never. I guess she was afraid…. Gee, I don't know how to … Where does she live?"

"On Riverside Drive."

"A swell apartment? Gee, I don't know."

"Listen, Mac," said Benny Chase. "Why not have Dolly bump into her by accident, just as she is leaving the apartment some day. We can find out when she goes out."

Dolly looked at him with growing admiration. "That's good, Mr. McQuirk. I could do that—an' act very surprised! She wouldn't suspect anything that way. And maybe she'd tell me things."

"Maybe she'd tell you things."

CHAPTER THIRTY-FIVE

Back in his own Newark office, Charley Phillips dictated a note to District Attorney Frisbee.

Dear Mr. Frisbee:

I think I can say without any reasonable doubt that the playing card you sent me was mailed from this city by a man known as Al Turner, a police character who is not well known here. Since he may be living here at present, however, I suggest that you send me a copy of his record, his fingerprints and photographs so that I may locate him and have him watched whether there is any cause for his immediate arrest or not.

It has given me a great deal of pleasure to obtain this information for you and I trust our delay—the letter was written thirty-six hours after the card had been received in Newark—has not inconvenienced you. If there is anything else we can do to help you we will be glad to do it.

Al Turner, as you probably know, was present at the murder of Clyde Poling in your city a little over a year ago, although he has not, to my knowledge, been questioned by your police department.

Sincerely,

Charles Phillips.

That was rubbing it in! He sent a duplicate of his letter to McQuirk, scribbling at the bottom: "For your own amusement. What can he say?"

Overnight his answer was back. The envelope contained the requested data and a very short note in reply.

Dear Mr. Phillips:

Quit stalling. How in hell did you find out who it was so quickly? Arrest Turner on sight and hold him until I can arrange to have him brought over here. Greatly obliged.

Yours forever,

Frisbee.

Now they had made it hard, sure enough. "Arrest" the man! Whew! McQuirk would have to be called on again. But he had the picture run in the local *Police Bulletin* and distributed to his men.

AL TURNER

Height 5' 11½"; weight 186 lbs.; hair: dark brown; eyes: brown—etc.; cocaine addict, usually armed, shifty eyed, walks with gait described as "lurching stoop".

But the man was not found in Newark.

Meanwhile Carl Denby was seized with an inward panic. He was getting in too deep with Frisbee. The Big Boy wouldn't like it. Lending him the card and the Newark envelope had been all right, but now he had taken Al Turner's record. No one knew what he wanted it for. Carl spent a sleepless night trying to decide if he should tell Martin about this activity now or wait. If he waited, and Frisbee took the bit in his teeth, he—Carl—would be the goat. He was acting against orders to release such data without reporting it to Martin. But how the man would rage and rail when he told him *now*. Which was best? Even deciding did not bring the dawn and when he finally got in to see the Deputy Commissioner the next morning, he was haggard and wan from his night of restless tossing.

"What's the trouble, Denby?" The fat man asked around an oily cigar. "You look like hell."

"I'm—I'm worried, chief. I—I got—er—"

"What is it?"

"Eh—Frisbee, he's …"

"What about Frisbee?" Martin never allowed anyone to finish a sentence without at least one interruption.

"Well, I did him a favor the other day. He asked …"

"What kind of a favor?" the cigar moved across the loose lips to the opposite corner of his mouth.

"He was workin' on a poison-pen case that …"

"*What* poison-pen case? I haven't heard anything about it."

"Well, that's what he said."

"Go on."

"He wanted to see those—er—those cards we got while Zim was here."

"Yes?"

"I let him have one …"

"You simpleton! When?"

"Day before yesterday; he …"

"Yes?"

"He sent it to Newark and found out that Al Turner sent it."

"Who's Al Turner?"

"He's a dope. A friend of Shields'."

Martin's little, pig eyes narrowed. "He found that out, eh? Then what?"

"He asked for Turner's record."

"You didn't give him that!"

"Yes, I did. Last night."

Martin's jaw clicked shut as he threw his cigar to the floor. "With *pictures*, I'll bet!"

"Why, yes…. He asked for 'em."

"You'd give him the gold out o' your teeth if he asked for it, wouldn't you? You lunatic! What do you suppose I've been doing all these months since—since Poling was shot? Playing ping-pong? Oh, get out! Get *out!* … No. Wait." Nervously, he lit a fresh cigar and paced the thickly carpeted room three or four times.

"Listen! You've almost thrown the fat in the fire. There's still time. Turner's in New York, not Newark. Find him. Find him, but don't pinch him. Just let me know where he is."

"Yes, sir."

"That's all."

CHAPTER THIRTY-SIX

The private detective combine of McQuirk, Chase, Melcher, Field, *and* Dolly Cushing, took turns at watching the apartment house on Riverside Drive, in pairs and singly. There seemed to be no routine to Patsy's days. One time she would leave early and return late, another time leave late and return early. It seemed impossible to time an accidental meeting of the two old chums.

Although they watched, from a safe distance, both night and day, Martin was never seen to come there.

"They meet somewhere else," McQuirk said. "Let Guy trail her tomorrow."

That day she had done a little shopping and returned to her home before Dolly could be located. The fourth day was Sunday. Pat might go to church, early. McQuirk was getting very impatient. Dolly met Benny Chase and they walked up the Drive together.

The big brown limousine stood at the curb. They quickened their steps and Patsy stood before them, her man holding open the door to her car.

"Patsy!" Dolly had no need to act. She was genuinely surprised. Despite her warning she was not prepared for the spectacle of elegance her old friend presented.

Patsy stood like a statue. The joy of recognition had lit her face, sent sparks from her eyes. Her beautiful mouth started to smile. Then the chauffeur coughed.

Her lids dropped, her little jaw set. "I—I fancy there must be a—a mistake," she said, and hurried past them, buttoning a glove.

Dolly was not to be denied. Heedless of the chauffeur, she clung to the door of the car, looking in at the gorgeous creature who sat stonily silent, staring straight ahead. "Patsy! Patsy, dear. Don't you know me? Don't you remember Dolly?"

"You—you mistake me for someone else, Miss. My name isn't Patsy." She had not dared to turn her eyes as she spoke. "Go on, Henri." The car started to move. Dolly dropped to the curb, sobbing.

CHAPTER THIRTY-SEVEN

Everywhere that the two detectives enquired for Al Turner, he had just left. He had been there that morning; he usually stopped in in the afternoon; he had been there yesterday or the day before; or—he would be around any time now. They waited here a while, there a while; they followed suggestions and clews all day long. They sat in Billy's over slow drinks for hours; he did not come. No one knew where he lived. He had left one cheap rooming house after another. He owed rent in several places and was not welcome back. Everyone seemed anxious to help the two officers. They would not tell Al that he was sought. If he came in they would all be glad to ask him where he was living.

While the search had been in progress, Al had gone over to Newark to buy some cheap snow. It was more than half salt, but it was cheap. New York prices had gone out of sight since Shields' death. The racket was shot. He got a three-ounce bottle in Jersey for two dollars. Cheaper than gin, that was, and twice as much fun. He locked himself in the men's room on the train and sniffed a quantity of the mixture. Not strong enough for that. When he got back he'd use his needle.

From the ferry house to the Bowery, every thirty to fifty feet an acquaintance, friend or creditor warned Al that the dicks were after him. At the fifth or sixth repetition of the news he became nervous. The street was dark. He bolstered his courage with a heavy sniff from his bottle. "It ain't even cut with salt," he complained. "That's sand."

He worked his way uptown, from barber shop to saloon, from restaurant to cigar store to saloon. In each place he was given the word. Between each stop he hit the bottle. By the time he reached Billy's he was in the clouds and half of his supply was gone.

Taxis were not fast enough for him. He could get along better on foot. Walking, he *flew*. His coat ballooned behind him and pedestrians stared. After him, were they? Well, they'd have to go some to catch him. Cops after him. After *him*. Huh! They'd get fat, they would. All he had to do was write a letter to Hoover. Old boy Hoover'd make it right with them. Or even the Prince of Wales. No use letting them surround him.

Billy regarded him across the bar with an evenly mixed feeling of disgust and pity. "You're high as a kite, Al…. You better get some sleep."

"Can't," said Al, scratching his nose and winking slyly. "Got a date to meet a fellow. He's coming here."

"Yeah? Two friends o' yours been here waitin' for you 'most all day. They were good customers."

"Not the same. This is an Englishman." He leaned across the bar and motioned Billy confidentially to him. "Secretary to the Prince of Wales," he said with an important leer. "Goin' to fix all this up for me."

"Oh, yeah?" Billy always humored them, no matter how they got that way. Dope was worse than booze, but if you humored them they stayed quiet, and quiet was necessary to the successful operation of a modern saloon.

"Expect him any minute—but, tell you the truth, I can't wait. When he comes, you make him comfortable. I'll be back."

"O.K., Al. We'll put him in the blue room."

The sarcasm rebounded from the shell cocaine had created. "That's the place, the very place," said Al. "And make him feel at home."

Bill shook his head as he shot the heavy bolts which shut his little bar from the general public. The lad was pretty far along. Two more sniffs and it would be the Queen of Sheba he was expecting.

Customers came, drank and went away. Some stayed and became heavier, lighter, profound or dull as their characters and personalities differed. Between the bar, the back room and the buzz of the door-bell, Billy was kept pretty busy.

A stranger rang for admittance. A youngish fellow with a soft red beard and a very English hat. Billy thought of Al's imaginary appointment. Funny. He let the man in. You couldn't make a living by being too particular. He found a table.

"Scotch and soda,"—and he actually produced amonocle. Billy went away chuckling to himself. "Secretary to the Prince of Wales"—that *was* funny. Was somebody putting something over on Al Turner? The man didn't look like a detective. Three scotch-and-sodas were consumed before Al returned. By this time his supply of the precious powder was almost gone—but it had not been wasted. Its effect was carrying Al to realms seldom before dreamed of by men.

Billy continued the joke. "Ain't that your friend, waitin' for you?"

"What? Who? Where? Huh?"

"Back of you. Ain't he the Prince's secretary?"

"Aw …"

"He ast for you."

"Oh, yes. So it is!" Al crossed to the stranger's table and sat down. Six or eight fellows at the bar turned to watch the crazy dope.

"Good evening," said Al. "I hope I haven't kep' you long."

"Oh, no," the other winked at Billy. "I didn't mind at all, don't you know."

"Huh?"

"Not at all; not at all. Eh—be seated. Eh—drinking, wot?"

"Huh? … Me? No. Never touch it…. Now, about this jam. Y' see, I'm the only one left. Y' see? An' I got the cards. Ha. See?" He displayed three playing cards. "That's what they want me for. That's why I sent for you. I—I knew you could fix me up, that is, the Prince."

"Eh—oh, yes, yes, of course, the—the—ah, Prince."

The man with the English accent studied the three cards closely. "Do they know you have these?" he asked.

"Know. My God! Of course. It's what they want. See? They want to burn me for killing 'im. But I never did it. It's the cards they want. They found out I had 'em."

"I see, an' you didn't kill him?"

"*Me!* Kill Poling? Of course not. But they're after me."

"Why don't you let me keep these for—eh—to show the Prince."

"Say! That's right. That's right. You, er, you show him, will you?"

The men at the bar were coughing and almost strangling on their drinks to contain their laughter. They nudged one another, and the door buzzer called Billy.

Two detectives, two tired detectives came in. A hush fell on the room. The Englishman had pocketed the cards. Something in the silence of the men at the bar warned him. He stood, winking at the officers. "Meet two friends of mine, Albert, old top! These are secret agents for the Prince. If you'll just step out with them …"

Al shook their hands without seeing them. "Oh, certainly, certainly."

They thought it best to use a cab to the station. He was goofy now. The wagon would set him screaming wild. And they were not supposed to pinch him. A cab was best.

The group had hardly left the curb in front of the saloon when the Englishman dashed out, hailed another cab, gave an address and was whisked rapidly away.

At the station, Al was thunderstruck! He gazed wildly about him, looking for space in which to fly. Carl Denby talked to Martin on the phone. "Put him to bed. I'll see him in the morning. And take his dope away from him. I'm glad you brought him in."

Carl was stunned at the unexpected praise. He did not remind Martin that it had been done against his orders.

CHAPTER THIRTY-EIGHT

Patsy's telephone rang. The hall boy stuttered. "A—a Miss Cushing to see you, Mrs. Train."

Dolly! Dolly had come—to call. To—to ask her questions. To chide her for being so rude, so cruel when they had met by accident. Oh, how had she learned the name? Couldn't she understand that it was impossible? Couldn't she see how it had hurt, had cut and torn her heart to refuse to recognize her? Didn't she know that old friendship could never be renewed now?

She was downstairs! What should she do? What *could* she do? The maid was out. Maybe—yes! She could beg Dolly to forgive her. To go away and never come back. To forget her—for all time. It would only take a minute. The boy was waiting.

"Send—send her up."

That was best. That was best. She could get rid of her before the maid returned. Dolly was sure to be reasonable. It would be good, *good* to see her again. A tap at the door; she threw it wide, her heart singing.

Behind Dolly stood Bert Melcher and McQuirk. "Dolly! You—you didn't bring friends."

"It's—it's Mr. McQuirk, Pat. He's going to help you."

Mac stepped quickly forward to forestall any tendency to shut the door. "We'd better get out of the hall, Miss Shelling. None of us want any publicity."

Patsy stood aside to let them pass. "Hello, Mel," she said wanly. "You in on this too?"

"We've come to get you out of it, Patsy. Dolly ain't doin' you no dirt."

"Oh, you don't understand, you people. I don't doubt your motives, Mel. Nor yours, Doll. But there's nothing to be done for me. I'm all right. If you'll all just go away and let me alone."

"Excuse me," said McQuirk, seating himself. "My corns are bothering me."

"Oh—eh—sit down, won't you?"

Mel found a chair. Dolly took Patsy's arm. "Oh, Pat, this place is lovely. It's just *adorable*, but you aren't happy here."

"Happy! Happy! Good God, don't ever say 'happy' to me. It drives me crazy."

Mac made a face at Mel. "Miss Shelling, we want your confidence. We must have it. Dolly has helped us. Mr. Melcher has helped us. Now, we want you to help us."

"Who is 'us'? You're not an officer any more, McQuirk."

"No, I'm not. I'm just a little bit better a man than when I was an officer. I've quit taking orders from crooks and I mean to move those crooks out of their offices. I'm being a citizen now, probably for the first time in my life."

"I'm not interested in politics."

"Neither am I. But I am interested in being a good detective. And so are half of the boys in the department. *More* than half of them. All they want—all I want—is a chance to do our stuff without crooked interference from over our heads…. Do you see what I mean?"

"Do you mean you are gunning for the man that fired you off the force?"

"*Fired* me! Who says he fired me? Does *he? Does* he? By the immortal … does he say that?"

"I don't even know who you are talking about…. Now, ladies and gentlemen, you will have to go. Thank you all—for everything. But you will have to go."

McQuirk shook his head. "Not until you answer a few questions, Patsy. We had a hard enough time getting in."

"If you don't leave this apartment at once, I'll call the police." She took a few steps toward the telephone.

"That won't do you any good, little lady. Our man is on the switchboard downstairs."

"Just wait until Happy hears of this!"

"Oh, you know Happy, then, do you?"

"I'll say I know him. And he'll put you—yes, all of you—in jail."

"Will you come to see us, like you did to see Zim?"

"Don't taunt her, Mr. McQuirk," Dolly expostulated. Patsy seemed about to snap. She was biting her lips, trembling; her hands fluttered like crippled birds, her eyes darted from one to the other of her tormentors. Dolly put her arms about her, but was shoved rudely aside.

"Listen, McQuirk. I'm not interested in a thing you have to say. I know where I stand. I've got the law on my side. You forced your way into my apartment—probably for blackmail. Now, I'll give you just two minutes to get out. Will you go?"

"Wait, Patsy," said Melcher, rising, "Mac is shootin' square with you. If you're on the level there ain't nothin' to be afraid of. We want you to train with us."

"Against the law? Train with you against the New York Police Department? Do you think I'm crazy?"

"But we've got evidence, Patsy. Loads of evidence. He's been crooked for years. All we need to have the police with us— is *you*. Happy has protected the Poling killer from the very start. If you'll tell us what happened that night, outside that door, we'll break him, and the whole force will be with us. Point of cold fact, you ain't got the Department back o' you. All you got is one crooked Deputy Commissioner."

"How do you know what I've got back of me? You can't prove that. And what the hell are *you* doin' on the side of sweetness and light, Bert Melcher? Seems to me, the last time I saw you you were on the other side o' the fence."

"Remember what I was doin' the last time you saw me, Patsy? I was settin' in a room with a lot o' fellows—doin' you a favor. Remember what we were there for, Patsy? Remember the Kid? How anxious he was to get out of town? Remember? Poling wouldn't be dead—if it wasn't for that meeting, Patsy."

"Poling! No! And the Kid wouldn't be in his grave today if it hadn't been for Poling either."

"Grave?"

"Is Chilton dead?"

"Yes, he's dead. You idiots! Do you think for a minute I'd be here, living like this if he was alive?" Tears were coming now. Her reserve was crumbling. For nearly two years she had dreaded some such meeting as this. Some such questioning. She had tried to prepare for it. Now it was getting her. She felt herself slipping. "Get out," she screamed. "Get out!"

McQuirk shook his head at Mel and Dolly. He had seen confessions come this way. He sat, apparently unmoved, and tried to calculate his next speech. "Did Happy tell you that?"

"Yes."

"I don't believe it."

"No?"

"No. I think he lied to you. He would, you know."

"I—I suppose so. But if he's alive why don't he come back? Or write? He's treated me like a dog."

"Now, now. There may be any number of reasons why you haven't heard. Maybe he don't like the way you've treated him."

"What was I to do? I didn't do it because I wanted to."

"Patsy, listen. We know everything. We've got millions behind us—and the newspapers. We only need one little link in our chain to send Happy Martin to the penitentiary."

"And me with him. Oh, *he* wouldn't go alone. No matter what you've got on him nor how many millions you have, he'll never go up the river alone."

"How can he take you? What have you done, Patsy? Did *you* shoot Poling—or Shields maybe?"

"No—oh—oh—God, no!" She ran away to her bedroom screaming, slammed and locked the door. Dolly ran after her, calling: "Pat. Pat, dear."

Mel and McQuirk looked at each other dejectedly.

"She's a tough one, Mel. I don't know how far we're going to get."

"I wonder if she's got a 'phone in there. She might be callin' the station." They listened at the door. Her sobbing continued without interruption.

"Listen, Patsy, we're going. I just wanted to say one more thing," McQuirk spoke through the door. "If we should prove to you that the Kid is still alive—would you come to our way of thinkin' then?"

The sobbing changed to a pitiful catching of her breath. The key turned in the lock. Mel, ever distrustful, slipped his gun into the side pocket of his coat and stood aside to watch the door crack widen. He was wrong. Patsy was quieter and very subdued.

"If you could find *him* or show me he was still alive, I'd—I'd tell you all I know. But unless he's alive, unless he's ready for me, maybe, to come back to him—I'm afraid. Oh, God, I'm afraid. *You* don't know. I—I couldn't ever talk unless I had some place to go to—right away. Somebody, like George, maybe, to—to…. Don't you see what I mean?"

"You're afraid of Happy and his friends? Afraid they'd get you?"

"They'd get me in a minute. If he went up—I'm telling you—I'd go too. If … my God! That's my maid. Please go. Please go now, quickly. She reports to him. The chauffeur reports to him. I'm watched every second. Please go—and—and you can come back, Dolly. Come back tomorrow at the same time. I want to talk to you."

CHAPTER THIRTY-NINE

By eleven o'clock the following morning Al Turner was in bad shape. He needed a pick-me-up and his bottle of yellowish powder was gone. Where the devil was he anyway? On a cot; cleaned of every penny, bottle, gun, letters, yes—even the last of the cards. All gone. He'd been robbed.

Funny room. Cot; blankets. Not jail, though—but look—bars on the window. He tried the door. It was locked from the outside. "Well, I'll be damned! I am in jail. This is one o' the bunk rooms back o' the office…. What'd they put me in here for? If I'm pinched, why not put me in a cell? Somebody in there always has a little snifter for a fellow when he wakes up like this."

He pounded on the door and listened. A chair clumped down outside and heavy feet approached. A key turned. "Hello, fellah. Feelin' better?"

"I feel lousy."

"Yeah. Y' want t' eat?"

"Eat? Naw. Say, what's this? Am I pinched?"

"You're detained."

"Huh? Is 'at some new name for it?"

"Martin wants t' see you."

"What's he want?"

"He didn't tell me."

"Can we get it over soon? Say, have you got my stuff somewhere or was I rolled?"

"We got it."

"Er—*all* of it?"

"Worried about that rod? Martin's got it. Go right in."

It didn't seem right to Al. *Go right in*—to Happy Martin's private office? He turned the knob with skeptical fingers and gave the door a timid push.

Martin had an elaborate breakfast spread on a small table at the left of his desk. He was slicing ham and chewing as the door opened. A trickle of yellow egg curved downward from one corner of his mouth. "Hello, Al," he said cordially between swallows. "Draw up and have an egg. I'll send for more toast."

Wonders—it now appeared—would never cease. On the plate-glass top of the Commissioner's desk lay Al's under-arm holster with his gun in it, his bottle, letters—in short, the contents of his pockets.

"You were pretty wild last night, Al. Come on, sit down and have a bite of breakfast."

"No—no, thank you, Mr: Martin. I can't eat so—-so soon after a—a drunk."

"Drunk?! *You*, drunk? Since when did they begin powdering whisky?"

"Well ..."

"Would y' like a shot o' that?"

"Gawd! Could I?"

"Sure…. But wait. Not that junk you've got there. In that case over there you'll find some of the real thing."

"You—you mean it?"

"Sure—help yourself."

In a cabinet across the room a complete and elaborate outfit lay ready at hand. Al's hands trembled so that he almost dropped the little square bottle.

Martin pushed his chair back from the table and turned toward Al. "Oh, Turner, before you start that—come here a second."

Al obeyed.

"Read that paper—and sign it."

Al read with difficulty. At first he struggled with the words themselves, then with the general import of the first few paragraphs. He had reached the middle of the document before he realized what it was all about. "You want me to sign this?"

Martin nodded. "Sign that, an' then take your shot."

"Oh," said Al. "I see. Sign it—or go without the shot."

"Well, I didn't say that."

"Is there anything else in it?"

"Meaning what?"

"Do I get anything else out of it besides one shot?"

"Sure. You walk out—a free man."

"Is that all?"

"Is that *all?*" Happy waved his hand at the relics on top of the desk. "Would you like to be booked for all this? Carryin' a gun; usin' hop; God knows what all? Would you like that?"

"I—well—I never thought you was ... well, what's the idea?"

"Look here, Al. I'm making a speech at the Woman's Club in twenty minutes. I ain't got time to bother with you. Sign that paper or in you go."

"Sign it—and out I go? Can I take my stuff with me?"

"Yes. I'll even let you do that. You can take that fresh stuff with you too. I ain't stingy."

"Give us the pen."

"Atta boy. Now, blow. Take this truck and get out of here. Get out of town. This will be in the afternoon papers."

As Al passed down the corridor he was surrounded by newspaper men. He tried to avoid them, tried to hide from their cameras. There were too many of them. Reporters and photographers were everywhere. A statement. They wanted a statement. What a fuss they were making. He wished he had read the paper through to the finish. What was all the noise about? He had nothing to say. At least four of the cameras caught good likenesses. Bewildered and angry, he finally gained the street. What did they take him for, a movie star?

A uniformed officer, an old crony of McQuirk's, caught his elbow. "Get in that car," he said. "And go with that fellow. He's got somethin' for you." Guy Field sat in the rear seat. Bert Melcher was driving. Al did not recognize Mel's back and he had never before seen Guy Field.

"Jeez," said Al, a little swollen with his triumph and the attention he was receiving. "Those guys get me sore."

"Nuisance," said Guy. "Damned reporters. Drive a man crazy."

When his driving permitted, Mel turned around and held out his hand. "How are you, Al?"

"Hello, Mel…. I ain't seen you in a coon's age. How's every little thing?"

"Good enough, Al. No kick. How's it by you?"

"Pretty good. I—I just had breakfast with Happy."

"Yeah? What'd he have to say?"

"Oh, nothin'. Passin' the time o' day. Swell guy, Happy."

"Swell," Mel agreed. "What's this great announcement he's going to make?"

"Oh, that. Well, I guess it's about a paper I just signed. I didn't read it all. Some old job they wanted me to clean up…. *You* were there; that Poling job."

"Yeah. I thought that was it. Happy had all the newspapers send men over. Said he had a most important announcement to make. So you signed a paper, eh? What was it?"

"Oh, nothin' much. It'll be in the afternoon papers. I ain't supposed to talk."

The car stopped before McQuirk's home.

"What's this?" Al asked suspiciously. "Where we goin'?"

"Come on in. It's a party. Happy says it's O.K."

"O.K. with me."

The three men entered the dimly lit room. Strong arms gripped Al from behind and he found himself disarmed, sitting on the floor. McQuirk grinned down at him.

"O.K., Al. Set up. That's all the rough house. Make yourself right at home. We're waitin' for a few friends."

CHAPTER FORTY

E xactly at the appointed hour Dolly called upon Patsy—Mrs. A. V. Train, as she called herself. But contrary to the terms of the invitation, Dolly was not alone. By her side was a tall young man with a soft red-yellow beard, a very English hat and the clothing of a London gentleman.

The door opened. "Hello, Dolly. Come—oh, you brought someone—*George!*"

"Patsy!"

Dolly had to push both of them through the ante-chamber to close the outer door. Then all three began to cry. Two of George's largest handkerchiefs were passed from hand to hand. The tiny ones of the two girls were ridiculously inadequate. They cried and cried and cried, stopping now and then to laugh, to embrace each other, to kiss or pat or stroke stray hairs back into place. For five minutes none of the three succeeded in framing a single articulate thought. Even Dolly, who should have been prepared for the meeting, was overcome by the joy of the other two. Finally they became calm enough to begin the interminable questioning that would continue for days.

In the meantime, Happy Martin had canceled his appointment to appear at a Woman's Club luncheon. Patsy's maid had turned in her report for the previous day. He had heard her through with scarcely an interruption. "A whole crowd of men—and a woman named 'Dolly'—eh?"

"Yes, sir."

"And Dolly's coming back today?"

"Yes, sir. I think she is there now."

"That's all." He got in his car. "831 Riverside Drive," he said. "And make it snappy."

PART FIVE

CHAPTER FORTY-ONE

"You're looking great, Pat. You've got a fine place—here." A worried look darkened the Kid's eyes a moment and was gone.

"It's a jail, Kid," Patsy said. "Oh, he told me you were dead. He brought home a Spanish paper and pretended to translate it—a piece about you dying of something, in South America."

"I ain't dead. I never was in South America. I went from Havana to Liverpool on a freighter. I been in England and France ever since."

"I know, now. Of course he was lying. But—but I didn't understand. I thought sure you'd write me at Dolly's hotel."

"I was afraid to write, Pat. Afraid I'd get you in trouble. After what happened on the way to the boat that night I got scared. When I got to Havana the American newspapers down there were full of the story. I had a hard time getting off the boat. Some fellows helped me."

"It was already in the papers when you got there?"

"It had been, for days. That freighter I was on crawled along like a snail. It gave me plenty of time to think."

"Oh, George…. Don't it, don't it truly make any difference? Are you gonna have me back again—anyway?"

"We're gonna get married before the sun goes down."

"Honest, Kid? Then let's get out of here, quick. That maid'll be back any minute—and she'll trail us. Oh, Kid, I don't want any more trouble. I never want any more …"

A key turned softly in the lock of the hall door. The maid would use the rear. "It's him. It's Happy! Beat it in there quick!"

Chilton dove for the bedroom door, followed by Dolly.

"Who's there?" Patsy called.

"Just me," said Martin grimly. He held his heavy walking stick like a club, well toward the tapered end. "Who's here with you?" His hat was pushed back, his eyes were bloodshot and wild.

"A girl friend, Happy. You've heard me speak of Dolly."

"I should say I had. What's she hiding for? Your guilty conscience, eh? You knew I wouldn't stand for any of those Broadway trollops up here."

"She's just leaving, Happy. It doesn't matter."

"How long's this been going on?"

"Only today.... I met her on the street."

"That's a lie." His back was toward the bedroom door. Chilton stepped quietly through it and stood, waiting for the mountainous figure to turn. "She was here yesterday too. Don't deny it. And God knows how many times before. Well, you know what I'm going to do now? I'm going to beat you within an inch of your life. I'll teach you to carry on behind my back." The sound of his own voice seemed to increase his rage. He bellowed the last few words and raised his cane to strike. Chilton caught it and sent it spinning across the room, at the same time throwing the other's fat left arm into a hammerlock. Entirely unprepared for this attack, Martin struggled to free himself. George felt the man's pockets swiftly. In his top-coat pocket he found a .38 caliber revolver. He started to hand it to Pat, changed his mind and slid it across the floor after the walking stick.

"Be quiet," said Chilton, "or I'll break your arm."

"Who is this man? Patsy! Do you hear me? Who is this man? Go to that 'phone and call the police."

Chilton looked over the fat shoulder and said quietly. "Put on your coat and hat, dear. Get Dolly."

Martin tried to turn around to see who was holding him. The Kid wrenched his arm still higher in the middle of his back. "Stand still, you fool. I'll break it." Patsy ran to her room.

"You'll pay for this! You idiot! I don't know who you are, but if you know me you'd better let go."

"Know you? Why, you dirty crook, everybody in town knows you."

"I'll put you in jail for the rest of your life."

"You'll put nobody in jail, Happy. You're done! Your goose is cooked. And as soon as these ladies get out of here I'm going to paste you in the jaw."

"Let go! Let go of me, do you hear?"

Patsy and Dolly returned struggling into their coats. "Downstairs, quick, you two. Take her to Mac's, Dolly. Stay inside, off the street, until I come there. And, Patsy, you do whatever McQuirk tells you. He won't steer you wrong."

"McQuirk!" Martin bawled. "McQuirk! Is this his idea? Why, God damn him, I'll have his hide! I'll burn him! I'll …"

"Shut up," said George, shoving the struggling blackguard away from him and releasing his wrist as he heard the door close behind the two girls. "You've burned your last man." His left caught the fat man's cheek and staggered him. His right went into his middle, and Chilton thought how remarkably like a pillow his stomach was.

Happy ran for the revolver on the floor but the more agile Kid caught him on the ear and sent him sprawling. "Get up! There's a lot more coming."

Then Happy tried to fight. Still he had not recognized his assailant. He put up his fists and tried to defend himself. George cut his knuckles on the fellow's teeth, bruised his other hand once more on his jaw. Martin backed away, around and around the room, now holding his open hands in front of his face, now punching futilely at the air where George had been but somehow never stayed.

A bridge lamp crashed. Happy's feet tangled with a small rug. When he would not rise, Chilton picked him up and propped him in a chair, and punched and punched again. The fat man lunged from the chair and tried to grip his tormentor's waist. Fists rained on his jowls.

The gun had been kicked from place to place so often that neither man knew where it was. Another chair crashed to the floor. Martin tore pictures from the wall and threw them, but the Kid kept coming on. Another picture—the glass spattered them both. Another—no, that was a mirror—he couldn't throw that. From room to room, all over the apartment, Happy was pursued by those puffed and bleeding hands, raising and lowering, raising and lowering, as monotonously as pistons—driving wit and sensibility, all but life itself, from his body—until Chilton's arms were weary, his hands numb from so much punching. Happy's face looked like raw liver. Blood streamed from his mouth and nose. He could no longer talk. He could not even stand. He rolled over and puffed in a battered pile at the Kid's feet.

Once more he set the fat man in a chair and again began a methodical drubbing of his features—but it became apparent at length that his blows were no longer felt. Happy Martin had ceased to feel. And, upon analysis of his own attitude, George found his spleen cooled and growing cooler each time his knuckles touched even that soft flesh.

Chilton found the revolver under the divan and put it in his pocket. Then, carefully, almost as if performing a surgical operation, he washed his battered hands—and put on his hat. The Deputy Police Commissioner had slid inelegantly to the floor.

"So long, Happy," the young man said. "I'll send the wagon up for you."

CHAPTER FORTY-TWO

he afternoon papers carried this story, with pictures of Al Turner:

ZIMBRONSKI KILLED POLING

"Eye-witness Martin" Obtains
Signed Confession from Eye Witness

Al Turner, Alleged Gangster, Tells All

Deputy Commissioner "Eye-witness" Martin, who earned that sobriquet through his ability to find reliable eye witnesses to acts of criminal violence, proved his mettle again today by obtaining a full, signed statement from one Al Turner, a police character who has been sought ever since the murder of Clyde (Boss) Poling. The story, which coincides with all of the details accumulated by the police through their prolonged investigation, lays Poling's death at the door of the notorious Mike Zimbronski, executed last May for the wholesale killing of five officers in the infamous Bronx Massacre. It was this slaughter of police and federal operatives which led indirectly to the murder of Poling by one of his own band.

The statement was obtained early today without duress, given voluntarily by Turner who had been apprehended the night before by Martin's men, acting on advice from his secret agents. Turner has been liberated on his own recognizances and has promised Commissioner Martin to be available at any time for further elucidation of his sworn statement.

This new development in the strange case will release the best brains of the police department for more concentrated analysis of the Shields' murder which occurred as an aftermath. It is thought at police headquarters that members of Poling's gang, thinking Jake Shields to be guilty of their chieftain's assassination, shot him in turn and deposited his body in the cellar of a burned building in Yorkville.

Heretofore secret information, released today, indicates that an accomplished surgeon was connected with Shields' murder since the bullet which killed him had been probed from his skull before an anonymous note informed the police of the body's whereabouts.

The complete text of the signed and sworn statement of Al Turner follows.

While this astounding news was being run through the presses of every newspaper in the city—except the *Register*—the millionaire publisher of that sheet sat next to McQuirk in the Mayor's office. The Mayor and District Attorney Frisbee faced the two men. The Mayor was speaking.

"I think you gentlemen have rendered this city a tremendous service. This is not the first time that the matter has come to our attention. We asked for Mr. Martin's resignation on the day of Poling's murder. But he promised to see that the corruption stopped. We thought he was sincere and we have given him a chance to make good.

"The facts which you have assembled if you are able to prove them—as you doubtless are—will be more than enough to remove him from office. We will discuss further prosecution at another time. I will have his resignation by midnight tonight."

The Mayor scowled thoughtfully. "I—I do not mean to imply that you have acted through any motive of self-interest, Mr. McQuirk, but it gives me great pleasure to offer his post to you, your incumbency to begin the moment I file Martin's resignation."

"Oh, well, now, Your Honor—I—I didn't—well, I'm not—"

"A man of your ability deserves what small rewards this department has to offer. You would make a splendid head of that department, the Chief Commissioner is a very old man…. Then, too," he winked at Mac, "you are very popular with the voters. I have yet to hear a word against you."

"It's no more than right," said the journalist, and States Attorney Frisbee nodded assent.

"All right. I—I accept. Thank you, Your Honor. I—I'll be waiting at my home for your summons to go on duty."

"Good-day, gentlemen."

The callers arose to go. "I'd like to break this story all over my front page in the final tonight, Your Honor. Have you any objections?"

"No—I think not. I'd like to have Martin in custody—er—that is—in the office, I should say, before he gets wind of this. He might do something rash."

"I'll start men out at once, Your Honor. We'll have him here by the time Mr. Scott's final edition is on the street," said Frisbee.

"It's all right then; go ahead."

"Will you be where I can get you later, Frisbee?" McQuirk asked. "I'm going to know who killed Poling and Shields in about an hour."

"You *are?!*"

"Sure thing. And I'll want your office to arrest someone."

"I'll wait for your call, Mac. By Heaven, you're a marvel!"

CHAPTER FORTY-THREE

Al Turner had paced the room every minute since McQuirk had left to join Scott in the Mayor's office. He had stopped when Dolly and Patsy arrived only long enough to exclaim with Mel at the dark girl's presence. Then he had started again. Finally Benny Chase led him to another room. "You do that zoo stuff in here, young fellah. We want to talk."

Patsy turned abruptly from the window. "Oh, Doll, do you really think he'll be all right—there alone with Happy."

"What's that?" Mel shouted. "Alone—who's alone with Happy?"

"George. He stayed in the apartment while we came on ahead."

"Good Lord! He shouldn't have done that."

Benny dashed to the 'phone.

"Who you callin'?" barked Mel.

"The department! Denby. It must be all right by this time. Somebody's got to stop Martin."

"What do you want to do, send Chilton to the chair?"

"Gosh, that's right. It's still up to us. Let's go, Mel."

"We can't both go. Somebody's got to stay here so Turner don't fly away.…. I'll go."

"No! Let me."

Mel clapped on his hat. "You stay here with the girls. And—better turn a key on that hop-head, too."

Their ways crossed, of course. Mel was urging his own car uptown as fast as traffic would permit, while Chilton fretted in a cab coming downtown, going to Mac's house.

The old westerner was none too soon. Reeling and more than half blind, Deputy Commissioner of Police—"Happy", "Eyewitness" Martin—stumbled across the side-walk and into his car. His chauffeur stared at him in amazement. "You're—you're hurt, sir."

"Drive—drive away."

Mel leaped from his car and entered the building. He grabbed the hall-boy's lapel. "Listen, son. Get a doctor, see? Get a doctor and go to Mrs. Train's apartment *at once!*" He did not wait to hear the boy's reply, but jumped back in his car and followed the limousine with its official license plates.

The boy was brighter than he looked. He went to the apartment himself and learned that Mel's fears were groundless, since a doctor could not mend the smashed furniture.

As the two cars roared out the Boston Post Road, Chilton entered McQuirk's apartment. His hands and wrists were swollen to almost twice their normal size and a vivid green and purple hue was spreading over their entire surface. Still he felt half defeated, because—after all—the affair could not be called a fight. It had been a one-sided slaughter.

Patsy bathed both misshapen paws with kisses. "Darling. Darling. Oh, George. I'm so glad. So glad."

They were interrupted by the arrival of McQuirk. "Hello," he said, obviously surprised at Patsy's presence. "Glad to see you, Patsy…. Good Lord, Kid, what've y' done t' your hands?"

"I been settling an election bet."

"You what?"

"He—he met Happy," said Patsy.

"He *met* Happy. Wow! I should think he had. And—is—is Happy still alive?"

"He was when I left him," Chilton grinned. "Here's his gun."

"What did you do? Take this away from him?"

The Kid nodded. "I'll say so. He was pullin' it on me."

"Where is he now?"

"I left him on the floor at Patsy's."

"Mel went up there, Mac," Benny offered. "He could be back, so I guess he's taking care of something. Trust Mel."

"Yeah…. Well, children. Your father … where's Al?"

"He's in the bedroom there, makin' out like he's a tiger," Dolly told him.

"Your father," the old detective continued, "and your humble servant, becomes Deputy Commissioner of Police tonight."

"You?"

"Aw, Mac, that's swell."

"Congratulations!"

"I told all of you that *first*, before any of you do any more talking. I want to be square with everybody. I want to do the right thing. Now, I'm goin' in and tell Al. I'll be in that room for thirty minutes. If there's anybody here when I come back out, it'll be because they *want* to stay. Get me?

"You, Chilton, don't need to worry about the Brown fracas. There's a train to Toronto or Montreal, I forget which, at eleven tonight. But I won't bother you with any of that.

"The front door's open. There ain't a cop within a mile. So long. See you all later." He had passed on into the bedroom before anyone could answer.

About thirty minutes later he came out, with Al Turner.

The house was deserted.

CHAPTER FORTY-FOUR

Melcher scarcely had time to apply his brakes, so suddenly had the car ahead changed its mind. It turned sharply around and started back to town at the same breakneck speed. "The man's crazy," said Mel, as he almost overturned, negotiating the same sharp about-face.

The two cars tore into town, not more than thirty feet apart. The unique horn of the Commissioner's car gave him all rights of way and Mel was so close behind that there was no questioning his right to proceed through the same paths.

They passed Patsy's apartment, a little slower. Two plain clothes men talked before the door. Martin's car leaped forward with a new burst of speed. Mel followed, suiting his gait to that of his quarry. They swung across town and went down Central Park West—to Happy's own apartment. Two detectives stood in the doorway. "Go *on*. Go on!" he shouted at his driver.

Through the park, around and around. For the better part of an hour they circled and doubled back and forth through Central Park, then, apparently the big car needed gas. It emerged from the park at 110th Street and halted at a filling station. The second pump at that stand was busy. Mel's hopes sank. Dusk was descending. They would be ready to start for Denver, with a full tank, while he could not last another hour at the pace they had gone. He took a chance on passing them and stopped at a rival station on the next corner. "Rush it, fellah. I'm in a hurry."

As the tank was being filled, Happy sent his chauffeur to buy papers. Before the man returned the fugitive took a pistol from the front door pocket and slipped it into his coat. As the car rolled away, he pulled the curtains down and turned on the ceiling lamp. One of the papers was the *Despatch* telling in bold type the story he had given them to tell, of his successful coup with Al Turner. The other was the *Register*.

MAYOR DEMANDS MARTIN QUIT

Turner Statement Spurious
McQuirk New Chief

Reign of Terror Under "Eye-witness"
Martin Ends Tonight!

Mayor Woodrow stated in an exclusive interview with a *Register* reporter this afternoon that he would have Deputy Commissioner Martin's resignation by midnight. The head of the city's Police Department could not be located as this paper went to press.

Acting upon facts placed before him by representatives of this paper and ex-Lieutenant of Detectives Jerome P. McQuirk, District Attorney Frisbee announced from the Mayor's office that he would know the name of Clyde Poling's murderer by nightfall.

It became known today, largely through the efforts of the *Register*, that Jake Shields had been killed by the same hand that slew Clyde Poling. It was said that Deputy Commissioner Martin had withheld from the Police Department and the District Attorney's office for months, facts which would have brought the guilty person or persons to a bar of justice.

Al Turner, reformed gangster, told a *Register* reporter that he did not know the contents or purpose of a paper he signed for Martin earlier today. This paper is said to have been foisted upon the public, as well as the Department of Justice, as a sworn statement of an eye-witness to the killing of Poling by Mike Zimbronski.

Special, extra editions of the *Register* will appear every sixty minutes all night tonight and all day tomorrow with the *exclusive* story of this series of crimes perpetrated under the direct supervision of the arch-villain Martin.

There will be *pictures* of the bullet which slew Shields. Photographs of the fingerprints of the man who fired Shields' gun and later left his body in a cellar on 80th Street, with nearly fifty thousand dollars in cash in the pockets of his clothing.

"Get out of the park," Happy said through the speaking tube. "Go east on 80th Street—until I tell you to stop."

Melcher's eyes widened and his breath escaped in a long, low whistle as he realized the course the limousine was taking. On this street, some four blocks away, was the ruin of a burned house.

CHAPTER FORTY-FIVE

Guy Field had descended upon McQuirk's household—in force. He had two photographers and an extra boy to carry plates. He had a man from a phonograph company with wax discs. "I'd put up a 'mike' and shoot this over the radio if I could," he beamed at Mac. "Gosh, this is a glorious day."

McQuirk looked on in stony silence. His lips were set hard. His eyes seemed to regard something at a great distance. From time to time he would rub his forehead. It didn't pay to be square, then. He had been wrong all the time. Give them an inch…. Once a crook, always a crook. But why had Benny Chase gone with them? Stuck on Dolly, maybe. He watched the men setting up their cameras as Al Turner repeated his story about the secretary to the Prince of Wales.

The door opened again and in they all trooped. Dolly, Chilton, Patsy, a stranger and Benny Chase. All close together, doing a lock-step. "Hello, Mac!"

"What's the matter with Mac?"

"He's all right!"

The old detective grinned like a school-boy caught in the cooky jar. They *were* his friends. He had not been wrong to trust them.

"Where—where you been?" he asked weakly.

Benny waved a document under his astonished nose. "We been buyin' a dog licen—no, no; a *marriage* license…. Who's all right?"

"*McQuirk's* all right!"

"Who?"

"McQuirk!"

"This is the minister," Dolly said, pushing the stranger into the crowded room.

"Gee, that's fine," McQuirk murmured.

Guy grabbed him. "Come on out here a minute and talk for this record. We're gonna give 'em away free with subscriptions to the paper."

"Have you seen Mel?" Mac asked a little helplessly as a flashlight exploded in his face.

It was necessary eventually to throw a cordon of uniformed men around the house to keep the crowds moving. After the ceremony had been performed and the principals photographed and re-photographed in every imaginable combination, it was learned, for publication, that the groom was not George (Kid) Chilton, but one "Albert Hohnson", a British subject, and all the captions were thus rewritten.

Finally the house grew quiet. A kiss from his bride had sent Chilton to the station very happy. He would wait for her in Toronto and together they would go to his new home in England. Al Turner had gone to the *Register* office with the boys. The police outside kept envious reporters from other newspapers from bothering McQuirk.

Patsy smiled at the big, tired man at her side.

"I'm ready, now. Where shall I start?"

"First, tell me who did it."

"Happy."

"Happy! Why didn't I think of that before? Of course it was.... Oh, you poor kid, no wonder you were afraid to talk.... Well—tell me about it."

"I spent all that afternoon at his apartment, trying to get it fixed for George to get on Shields' boat. He finally consented.

Then Frisbee and Woodrow came out there themselves and told him he had gone too far. He had told Poling about the police going to stop his truck—and Poling was riding the truck that night. The Mayor and Frisbee told him to arrest Zim or resign.

"He said he would. He was very frightened. After they left he rushed past me to the street. I followed him and he said he was going to arrest somebody to keep the boys quiet.

"I saw he meant George. He was going to double-cross him. I knew where they were, but he had to go and find out first. I got there ahead of him and took the Kid with me. At the corner we almost ran into Happy, talking to a whole crowd of policemen and detectives. I saw them just in time to get George in a cab, then I went up to him.

"I'll admit I hated Poling. You can't blame me, Mac. He was responsible for what the Kid did. If it hadn't been for him, George'd be honest and clean today. So I said: 'Mr. Martin, do you want to know where your man is?' And he said: 'Yes.' So I said: 'You come alone and I'll show you.' He walked a couple steps with me and says: 'If you're double-crossin' me, Patsy, I'll kill you.' But I finally convinced him it was on the level. I—I didn't know what might happen to him. I didn't care. But he figured that all crooks were his friends; that he could go anywhere. I guess he intended to warn them all. I don't know. So much happened. He sent the police away. He said: 'Scatter, you guys. I'm goin' to handle this alone.'

"We got in his car and drove down the block to that entry. I went through first. He waited until I got to the door, then he followed. You know how that place is; one door *here*, another one facing it, and the steps to your left. Well, as I stepped in, the door right at the top of the stairs opened and a man came out. It was Shields. Just then Happy came in behind me. When he saw

Shields he ran up the steps ahead of me. He had his hand in his pocket but I don't think he had a gun.

"'Hello, Shields,' he said. 'Who's in there?' 'None of your business,' Shields said. 'Get out o' here, cop,'—and he pulled his gun.

"I don't know how Happy did it, but he tripped him some way and got the gun. They were struggling for it when it went off. I was too scared to move. I didn't know any shots went through the door, but they must have."

"Yes—we've thought for some time that Poling was killed accidentally. Go on, child."

"Shields rolled all the way down the stairs. Happy dropped the gun and ran to him. 'Help me carry him,' he said. 'We'll take him to a doctor.' He didn't know he was dead. Not yet. Neither did I.

"We put him in the car and Happy made me drive. I don't know where the chauffeur was. Inside getting a drink, I suppose. Happy sat in back with Shields. We had only gone a couple blocks when Happy said: 'My God, Patsy, he's dead.' At the next corner, he said: 'I've got to get this thing out of here.' Just then we passed that burned house. There wasn't anybody on the street. He told me to stop. He went in and looked around and came back to the car. 'Turn out the lights,' he said. I did. Then he carried Shields into that house. I didn't dare leave him, even then. I knew how crooked everything was and I figured I was safer with him than with anybody else—and I wanted the Kid to get to Cuba.

"Happy was too nervous to drive. He made me. Next day he made arrangements to go away. You know the rest. I've been with him ever since. Neither one of us knew that Poling was dead until we read it in the morning papers. I was sorry for him, then, and for Dolly.

"That must have been terrible for a fellow like him—dyin' without a chance to defend himself. Dolly was crazy about him. She didn't know how bad he was, but I did."

"Poor, poor child.... Well, your troubles are over now. I'll get Frisbee to try to convict him on the strength of the fingerprints, if they tally, without calling you to the stand.... You'd better get some sleep now. Benny and Dolly can take you down to her hotel."

"Gee, I wish I was going to Toronto tonight."

CHAPTER FORTY-SIX

A sleek and well-fed Belgian shepherd dog romped on the sidewalk with a little girl in a very fluffy dress. With his mouth full of rope he growled and pulled while her baby laughter tinkled and pealed. Finally, in full possession of the rope, he shook and worried it back and forth, the baby in squealing pursuit. Her small arms encircled the great chest, and inadvertently her fingers touched the long white scar that a bullet had made. The dog winced, drew away and whined. That spot was very tender and it ached like an old man's rheumatism just before a rain.

The baby's mother appeared at the door. "Come in, Luella," she called. "It's dark now."

"Can't we play a minute more? Just a minute, mamma?"

At that moment an enormous limousine roared to a stop across the street. A hatless figure stumbled from the rear of the car. "Get out," he yelled at his chauffeur. "Go back to the garage." The baby, the mother, the dog stood transfixed, watching this wild creature. The car started away. The man turned toward the forbidding shadow of the burned house. A shiny, steel object glinted in his hand. Another car drew up and parked at the curb just as the figure disappeared in the charred doorway.

The big dog started across the street on velvet pads. His feet rose and fell with machine-like precision. He went through the twin beams from Mel's headlights and the ex-ranger gasped. Fate was taking a hand in this drama—at last.

"Go to it, boy," he murmured. "It's your battle, after all."

Like a wraith, the muscular dog slipped through the first dark room—the second. Happy stood at the edge of the hole in the floor. His blood roared so in his ears that he was deaf to all other sounds. Then the animal left the floor. Happy screamed. He lost his revolver trying to keep out of the hole. The dog's fangs found the short, pudgy neck and blood gushed into his mouth. Little bones cracked and crunched between his mighty jaws. The hands which had tried to ward him off grew quiet, clutching little wisps of hair.

Mel sat perfectly still in his car. His mind was in a hospital room where a border pal lay dying. "You knew where to place your bets, Slim," he whispered. "I'd go out myself for a dog like that."

Then from the dark depths of the ruin a cry—half bay, half howl—rose in a soaring crescendo toward the stars. It was repeated three times before the beast left his kill and returned to his dainty little playmate.

After a very cursory examination, Mel walked over to the baby's mother. "I'd keep that dog chained in the house for a few days, Mrs. He's just now evened up an old score of his.... Can I use your phone?"

"Why—why certainly."

"Mac?"

"Yes, Mel!"

"Happy's dead."

"No!"

"In a million years y' won't guess who got him."

"No? Who?"

"Shields' dog."

"The hell he did! ... Where?"

"In the burned house."

"Honest! ? Well, what do you know about that?"

"I guess there won't be any use workin' on the fingerprints any more now."

"Hell, no! There won't even be a trial. Oh, boy, *that's* a break. Now Patsy can catch that train…. Listen, Mel. Drive to Grand Central, see? Find Kid Chilton. He's around there, or will be. Tell him to get *two* tickets to Toronto instead of one."

"O.K., boss, I'll find him."

"And, Mel …"

"Yes."

"If I don't see you again tonight—I'm going to be pretty busy—come down to my office in the morning. I want to see you."

"Office? Whadayamean?"

"Down to the station…. I'm Deputy Police Commissioner."

"Yeah? … And I'm mayor. Come on out to the booby-hatch and see me."

"No, it's on the level, Mel. Is it true that you was one time a Texas Ranger?"

"Yeah—what about it?"

"We're gonna start a New York Rangers, see—and you're the boss."

Those gulls which followed the *S.S. Bantok* out of the Canadian harbor, bound for Plymouth, were not fooled by the small shower of white objects Chilton scattered over the rail. They were not edible. The Kid dropped the last fragment of the three playing cards from his bruised fingers and went below to join Pat. A ship's page pounded the gong for dinner.